The Greatest Most Traveling Circus!

Sweet Candy Press
Olympia Washington USA
2014

The Greatest Most Traveling Circus
Jonas

First printing
ISBN-10:0989709833
ISBN-13:978-0-9897098-3-5
Copyright © 2014 by Jonas

Sweet Candy Press
PO Box 13201
Olympia, WA, 98508

www.sweetcandypress.com

This is a work of fiction. Names, characters, places, and incidents either are the product of the author's imagination or are used fictitiously, and any resemblances to actual persons, living or dead, business establishments, events, or locales is entirely coincidental.

Front and back cover layout design by Sarah Frankie Linder. Back cover artwork by Ramsey Beyer.

The passage from Cindy Crabb's *Doris Encyclopedia*, used in the story "Love Me Nicky Ocean" was used with permission.

for Eric and Astrid

volume one:
"friends"

by jonas

acts...

The Greatest Most Traveling Circus

My uncle Havel lived out of the country; he only came around about once a year. When he came to visit, he'd stay with us for a few weeks, usually during the summer. During those weeks, everyone in the family wanted to see him, and then a skijillion other people were eager to see him too; he was this famous Czech scholar and wrote lots of books. But no matter how many people lobbied for his time, he always reserved his mornings for me. We went out for walks, just the two of us, every morning he stayed in town. We'd start from the house and walk all the way to the forest preserve at the end of the neighborhood, then back. Sometimes, we were both totally silent, during the whole walk. Sometimes he was silent, and only listened to me talk. Other times, I was silent, and made an effort not to smile too much while he was talking. It was better than any holiday. It was my favorite time of the year.

Well, one time (when I got to be around *that* age), during one of our walks, I asked Uncle Havel if he believed in God. He said ah, well now, let me think. God? I wonder. Yes. I will tell you this. I believe in the greatest, most traveling circus.

I asked him what that was. He explained.

When we die, Hannah, our souls stand up out of our bodies, and they wander. We do not know where we are going. We are very confused. But then, then we hear a noise. It is music. It grows louder and louder. And then! We see. It is a big party. A band. No, a parade. It is traveling somewhere, somewhere wonderful.

5

These people, in the parade, they play the trumpet, the guitar, the accordion, the violin, the drums, the trombone. They play every instrument. If they cannot play an instrument, they sing. If they cannot sing, they dance. If they cannot dance, they clap with their hands. They are all part of the music; all playing, laughing, and traveling. You recognize some of them. Some of them are the friends you have known. Some are your own blood. Also, then, you see that some of them, they are your enemies. But! Just as you see them, you cannot remember why they were supposed to be your enemies. What was the reason for this hate? Could it have been so terrible? You see them laugh, so full of spirit, so much bliss, and you can not find a reason to hate. With no apology, they are close to your heart again. They are like your blood now. They share your soul.

You join the circus, then. You climb up onto a horse, or an elephant, or a giraffe. Or a caravan. Something like this. There are also cars and trucks. Above, in the air, there are balloons and planes. You are all going to the same place, to the most wonderful place, where you shall be happy for eternity. This place, it is The End. The perfect End, where all of the marching stops. You, you are all filled with joy; you overflow with it, thinking about how perfect it will be. And this is why you all sing, why you play the song. Ah, Hannah, now I am wondering. Do you still practice the accordion?

I had been slacking on the accordion, majorly slacking, but still I nodded. Mmm-hmm.

Uncle Hav clapped his hands together and said, this is good! This is very good to hear! Then, at the parade, you will be given an accordion. By then, you will be a master. I am sure of it. You and I, my niece, we will play together. My violin will sing with your accordion. It will be marvelous. Marvelous!

So there! You have joined; you march in the parade. And the song does not stop, and you do not stop marching. Every minute, every second, more people are joining the circus. Animals join. Creatures you do not recognize, they also join. And they all become happy. They take up instruments and they play. So many, so very many have already joined. It seems to you, ah, yes, there must have always been this parade. Surely, it must have begun with one man, and before him, there was no parade. But you can see no beginning and no end to the parade line, though certainly there must be both. Or perhaps not. It does not seem to matter when it began, or if it began, because it continues, and continues and continues. What matters, is that you march. Always this. So you do this, you march with this greatest, most traveling parade. You march over hills, over mountains and plains. You march through the seas, both under them and over them. Because it makes no difference, you are all souls, no longer trapped in bodies. You see? The water is the same as the land now, the same as the air. It is all the same. You travel into the sky, through the clouds. The parade grows and grows.

Wait, I asked, is it a parade, or a circus? Uncle Havel said, it is as you like. The parade for a circus. A circus with a parade. Something like this. Call it what you wish. I will call it a circus. I nodded. I think so too. It should be a circus. I like circuses more than parades.

7

Uncle Havel nodded, and clapped his hands together. We agree, then. A circus!

And you must see now that this circus, it is never stopping. You march always, you sing always. You never grow tired because this, this being tired, it is only what souls do when they live inside weak bodies. You never forget about The End because every moment, new people are joining the circus, and every moment the circus is more complete than before, and so, the song is more full and rich.

And do you know, do you, that you will never reach The End? You must never. Because everyone must join the circus first. No one must be left out. If one person were left out, then you could not be happy. If one person were left out, you would look around and think, ah, but where is my dear friend? I cannot be at peace, because one of my friends is not here. This friend cannot feel what I feel. If all your friends were there, then you would worry this way about your family. If all your friends and family were there, then you would worry about strangers. These strangers, they would become your friends if they knew you, if they met you only once. And so you must be sure, yes, that every person is included. Everyone must join the march to The End. No one is being left behind, as we like to say. So of course you may not stop marching, not ever, not until every last creature in all of creation has joined. But even then, even then it would be best not to reach The End, because, just think, think of how joyous this is, to travel, only travel! It would be a shame to stop. You would say, ah! It was so much lovelier when we were marching! You would say this. You would grow bored, or restless. You would wish to turn around and march back to The Beginning.

And so, you must not stop. It would not do, this stopping. You must not stop!

And that, said Uncle Havel, is the greatest, most traveling circus.

I thought about it. I frowned.

But what about God, I asked. I asked if you believe in God? But Uncle Havel only smiled, and looked ahead at the trail. Then he spread his arms out wide and began to sing in Czech.

That night, I told my mother about it. I told her what I had asked him and then how he had answered. I tried to say everything just like I heard it, but it didn't sound as good as when Uncle Havel told it. But I tried. Before I had finished my mother stopped me. You poor thing, she said, holding back a grin. Really, Hav is too much. I asked her what she meant and she said, your uncle pulled a fast one on you, sweetie. He always says the opposite of what he means.

I still didn't understand, and my mother could tell. She said, your uncle is a very clever, very cynical man. If you ask him a yes-or-no question, he'll say yes, but only because he wants you to figure out on your own that the answer is really no. He wants you to believe that you've found the answer all by yourself. He's always been that way.

I thought about it for a long time. It's been well over twenty years and I still think about it. Both Uncle Havel and my mother have left to join The Greatest Most Traveling Circus, along with my grandparents, my niece Angie, a few friends, and a skijillion people that I never had a chance to meet.

Sometimes, I believe what I want to believe. Sometimes I believe what I think Uncle Havel wanted me to believe. Sometimes I don't care either way, and the truth seems very unimportant. And then I go and practice my accordion.

My Monster

The homework is to write an essay about a pet. I do not have a pet but I used to have a monster. She was great. She was as big as a truck and maybe bigger. She was the same color as the sky. She had big and sharp yellow teeth and she also had long yellow curly horns in place of ears. Even with horns and no ears she could hear very good. Her eyes were as big as plates and they were red. Her hands and her feet were like elephant feet and her hands were also like elephant feet and it was hard for her to hold anything. She had a big fat jelly belly. One thing that was that she did not have private parts. She said that she did not need no private parts because she did not do any of the things that private parts are good for. She was also bald, all over. She did not have hair nowhere on her body.

Her name was Stinky. I gave her that name because she was stinky. She smelled like number two and it was so bad. If you smelled her you would have said she needs to take a bath, but it was OK because that was just how she smelled. It was not her fault.

Stinky hid in the basement at my house. It is not my house it belongs to my mom. My mom did not know that Stinky lived with us. I tried to tell her about Stinky, but she only laughed and said I was being silly. No one could see Stinky but me.

Stinky was a girl like me, even though she was so much bigger than me. She ran away from home because her mom and dad are really mean. Stinky's mom and dad like to scare little kids. Also they eat little kids.

Stinky said eating little kids is wrong and also they taste funny. She said she would never ever eat little kids and she would never scare them either. This made her mom and dad upset. They yelled at her and yelled at her and then she ran away.

When I saw Stinky hiding in the basement I was scared. But then she told me not to be scared because she does not like to eat no kids. I wasn't sure but then I was sure. Then we were best friends.

Stinky was super nice but she had a bad temper. Stinky and I were playing in the basement and we stopped playing when we heard my mom and Doug-o yelling. They got louder and louder and then we heard a CRASH and then everything was quiet. Stinky and I went upstairs to see what happened. Doug-o was gone and there were broken plates and glasses all over the floor. Mom was also on the floor and she was bleeding and not moving. I started to cry.

Stinky got so mad she stomped out of the house and went to get Doug-o. I did not see her again until the next night.

Mom got better. She needed stitches but they came out after two weeks. Doug-o did not come back to our house. Mom thinks Doug-o broke up special times with her. Stinky would not tell me the truth but I knew she did something bad. All she said was she did not eat him.

There was one problem. It was not good for Stinky to live with me. She said monsters should not live where people live, because people air is icky and not good for them.

It is OK if they show up one time or two, but then they have to go back to places with special air.

Because of our icky air she had problems breathing. Her breathing sounded like bubbling water. I told her to see a doctor but she said nothing can help her she had to go home. She would not go home because then her mom and dad will yell at her and make her eat little kids for sure. She said if she has to do that she would rather just go away forever.

She is gone now and it is sad. Sometimes it is too sad and I want to also go away. My mom sees I am sad all the time and she asks me what is wrong. I can't tell her the truth and so I make things up. She thinks it will cheer me up if we get a dog or a cat. I don't want no dog or cat because that is dumb.

The only thing in the whole wide world that cheers me up is every time I am in the bathroom and I go number two there is the bad smell and it is just like Stinky is in the bathroom with me. Maybe that is sicko to you but it is the only time I am happy.

Any Old Idiot Can Get Himself Famous

I knew this guy named Viggo. Big hairy sucker. Take one look at Viggo and that was all you needed. He was another fly on the wall over at Binky's, this bar near my place. He was always drunk and suspect-looking. Sat by himself at the bar. But one day for no damn reason he turned to me and said wanna see something? I was bored and ain't had enough to drink yet so I said yeah sure. We got up and went out to the parking lot. It was dark and still and I thought, he's gonna try some bullshit. But then instead of trying some bullshit he went over to the nearest car, a beat up Dodge, and said watch this. He took a deep breath, bent down and with both hands grabbed the sucker by the fender and lifted it clean off the damn ground. He raised it higher and higher until his arms were over his head and the car was a good six feet up. Then he let 'er go and the Dodge fell back down on the asphalt. Ain't that a motherheifer, he said. I said that yes, that's a motherheifer all right. We went back in for another round. After his first drink Viggo said ain't it screwed up that I can do that and don't nobody freakin' know? Oh I know what you mean, I said, take a look at this. And I took the ballpoint out of my pocket and started doing calligraphy on my napkin. *Ain't that a motherheifer,* I wrote. That's pretty good, said Viggo, I like the f, that's a freakin' good f. I told him, I used to study calligraphy and now I can write it perfect and it won't get me not a goddamn thing. Viggo shook his head and said, know what? Sometimes I think, if everybody's a little bit special, ain't nobody special. I said right on, brother, and drank my beer.

14

A little after that, Viggo stopped going to Binky's. Years later, he was all on the goddamn newspapers, TV, magazines—everywhere. They didn't call him Viggo; turns out, he was some kind of super guy, even though in every picture, wasn't no doubt about it, he was just as chunky and hairy and Viggo as ever. It was all screwy, cause it meant that any old idiot can get himself famous. But it also made me smile, cause it meant that *any* old idiot can get himself famous. A little while after, I started doing my calligraphy again. I still do it now, just not as much, not since Martha passed away. But once in a while I'll take some scrap paper and my good pen and write 'any old idiot can get himself famous' in different ways. I can do it freehand and everything. Even on blank paper. The best part is the Gs and Fs. I'm the King of Gs and Fs. You want Gs and Fs, I'll show you some Gs and Fs. But you probably won't never see them. That's the screwed up part.

Little Man, What Now?

My nephew Heinrich used to be such a pain in the butt. He was a child prodigy; "Famous at Five." That would have been wonderful if he hadn't been so damned smug. There's nothing worse than a smug kid. I hated going to visit my brother; I was *bound* to see that little stinker. It was inevitable.

He was short, bony and pale as a ghost, with dainty little hands and a face that looked painted on. His regular expression was… melancholy. I don't use words like 'melancholy' too much, but with that kid, 'sadness' just don't quite hit the spot. You know how it is. Nervous juvenile, won't smile. That could be what screwed with me the most, because I swear to God, he looked like he had thoughts that I didn't know nothing about until I hit thirty.

His name isn't even Heinrich, really. It is now, but it wasn't supposed to be. My brother and his wife named him Henry. Henry Reich is on his birth certificate. But when he was three, Henry decided that his name ought to be legally changed—after his favorite German author.

During a visit, I'd see him off sitting in a corner, staring out of a window. Once, I tried reaching out to him. I said, hey chum, why so glum? He looked at me without saying nothing. I can't explain it well enough, but it's like he rolled his eyes at me without lifting his eyebrows. *Weltschmerz*, he said, then turned back towards the window.

I'll admit it, I didn't know what the heck that word meant. I looked it up in the dictionary, and when I couldn't find it there, I searched the Internet. It's good that I did too. I'd thought it was a made-up word. It sounds made up, don't it? You know how these kids are. When I was his age, I made up words all the g-dang time. *Scragglypoof. Wubblewop.* But the kid wasn't pulling my leg that time. Sure as shit, *weltschmerz* is real alright. Look it up.

The next time I came around to visit my bro's place, when I saw Heinrich padding on out of his bedroom, I said hey slugger, how we handling that *weltschmerz*? I think I must've pronounced it wrong, because he stopped, gave me this embarrassed look, shook his head, and walked away.

My bro and his wife were no help. They were bright folks, as far as that goes, but they weren't no Oxford scholars or nothing. From the jump, Heinrich was running the show. And it wasn't fair for them; everyone expected them to be geniuses, just because of the kid. So logic said, Pete and Dana must have passed down all the smarty genes. How can anybody live up to that? Around the time that Heinrich was whizzing by all those tests, breaking records like nothing, interviewers were constantly invading the house, firing away. What sort of prenatal diet did Dana maintain? Did she give birth naturally? The Bradley Method? Did she play record-ings of Mozart symphonies and press her belly up against the speakers? Pete and Dana usually didn't know how to answer those questions. Most of their responses were short and not too quick on the take.

Every so often, something they said came back to bite them in the butt—like when Dana had an interview on TV and said when she was asked where Heinrich's brilliant mind came from she said, *well, um, Pete used to take a lot of Gingko Biloba. A whole lot. More than normal. So there's that.*

As to why Heinrich was always so melancholy, Pete and Dana were as clueless as anybody. Don't ask us, said Pete, we just put food on the table and try to stay out of his way.

But, I said, don't you get sick and tired of Liberace strutting around here like he does? Dana shook her head.

We don't give him a reason to turn on us. Besides, to tell you the truth, we don't see him that much. He's gone most of the time, taking tests, giving lectures and demonstrations, consulting with doctors, therapists, specialists—the whole nine. When he's actually home, he keeps to himself and reads all day.

But come on, I said, he has to get on your nerves, a kid like that.

Pete me handed a beer.

Let me wax nostalgic for a jiffy, he said. This happened when Heinrich was three. He came running and screaming into our bedroom in the middle of the night, hopped right into bed with us. One in the morning. He was crying his eyes out. I asked him what was wrong and he said, *ennui.* He cried for hours before he finally fell asleep. We thought we were going to have to take him to ER, he was such a mess. Jesus man, are you hearing me? *Ennui.*

I only know what that means because I had to learn it for the GRE. And here he is, my three year-old son, having panic attacks over it. I swear to grandma's grave, Kurt, that boy is the Messiah. Or the Antichrist. One of the two. Either way, I'm not going to piss in his cornflakes.

Dana felt the same way. In general, they both believed that Heinrich was either going to kill himself or change the world. Me, I wasn't sold so easily. Anyone could tell that the boy was smarter than your average bear. Fair enough. What I didn't get was—what's so great about being smart? Growing up, I knew plenty of smart kids. They got picked on all the time. That's what being smart got them. First prize for the smart kid? An ass whooping after school. Second prize? An ass whooping after school. Go ahead and guess what the third and fourth prizes were. And even the smartest smart kid couldn't save himself from a good old-fashioned ass whooping. Every smart kid got a slice of that pie. And now, thirty something years later, all of those smart kids are grown up and out here busting their humps, just like the rest of us dummies. A few of them are even working for the same guys that used to make them eat dirt.

That's probably why, in spite of myself, I started getting more and more sarcastic around Heinrich. He brought out the bully. The mean booger in me was just dying to give him a wedgie. Toss him in a dumpster.

During family dinners, at the dining table, I'd glance over, see him sitting there all dark and pouty, and make some smartass remark like, whoa, somebody put a lid on this chatterbox over here! Ha ha! Pipe down, grasshopper, no one else can get a word in! You're hogging all the air!

19

That gab-gab gabbing of yours.

Heinrich would just look 'spiritually wounded' and ignore me.

I laid it on pretty thick. Thicker with each visit. Then, one Thanksgiving, I crossed the line.

It wasn't even one of my best jabs that got to him. It was just the straw that broke the camel's back. At the dining table, I asked if Baby Einstein needed some more brain food. He carefully set his napkin down on the table, and excused himself from the room. Well that made me the big louse. I'd gone and ticked off the golden goose. The whole table went quiet. Everyone looked at each other and looked at the table and didn't look at me. I went after the boy.

I found Heinrich standing in the doorway of his room. His arms were folded.

I find your behavior towards me intolerable, he said. *Explain yourself.*

I'd come with the intention of apologizing, offering to buy him a bike, some toys or something. And if he'd been crying, or called me a big meanie-head, I probably would've gone easy on him. Apologized even. But the way he said it, *explain yourself.* That rubbed me the wrong way. The gloves came off.

Oh I'll explain alright, you snotty son of a bitch. I'll explain real good. You don't know dick. You never had to pay alimony. You never had to buy a new carburetor for a piece of junk car that ain't even paid off yet.

You never got laid off work, never had to think really hard about whether you want to go get tanked, drive your car into a telephone pole, or both. You never stayed up all night in a hospital room, just so you could sit next to the bed and be there to hold your buddy's hand when he dies. Look at me. Look. This is the pain of the world. Right here. This face here. You little shit.

I could'a gone on and on. Maybe I did, and I just don't remember. I do remember the look on his face after I finished. His eyes bulged out the sockets. His bottom lip was shaking. If he was pale before, he was damn-near invisible now. But it wasn't just shock. It was shock and terror. He was scared stiff. I'd never seen him that way before. His whole face said, *you mean… this life… gets even worse?*

I felt like a heel. I was scared that he'd go and kill himself, just because I called him out on being a pompous little twerp.

I didn't see him for a long time after that. Pete and Dana said he slipped into a deep depression. Deeper than the usual kind. Now he was giving all his therapists the silent treatment. Everyone thought it'd be for the best if I didn't come to visit anymore. It totally ruined things between Pete and me. Man, that hurt so bad. Pete wasn't just my brother, he was my best friend. That's a corny thing to say, but he was. I had to practically give up watching baseball; Pete was my partner in crime and I couldn't call him up to bitch about the Cubbies. At first he was just really curt, but I guess as things got worse with Heinrich, he got more resentful, and at one point he stopped answering my phone calls. Dana too. They couldn't forgive me for taking off my kid gloves around their kid. Suppose I can't blame them.

I had to play telephone with the family to get news about them. I found out that Pete landed a job at a plant in Florida. Tallahassee, roundabouts. Packed up the kid and the missus and moved on down there. That was sixteen years ago.

All that time, every day, I checked the papers. I searched online. I watched the news, morning and evening. I just knew I was going to hear something about the kid. I wanted to start a scrapbook for him, keep track of everything. Nobel Prize. Pulitzer Prize. Discovery of a cure for cancer. Breakthrough in quantum physics. The key to the city, any dang city. Anything. I had dreams about making it into a biography, a real book. Getting it published. A bestseller. *My Nephew, The Super Genius.*

I looked and looked and looked. His name never popped up anywhere.

Then he came back.

There's an all night pub and grill down the street from the factory. It's a fine spot to hit on a break, or right after a graveyard shift. After filling in for one of my co-workers, on the way home I stopped in for a quick brewski. There he was, sitting up at the counter, drinking whiskey sours.

Heinrich's build was the same and even his height was about the same, but he wasn't pale and he wasn't delicate. I wasn't sure it was him, right away. I stared from across the bar for almost twenty minutes before I could tell. It took another twenty minutes to work up the nerve to go on over to talk to him. When I did, he got off his stool quietly and gave me a hug. It was all respect, that hug.

No affection. He didn't act surprised to see me. I wondered if he'd seen me there before, and just didn't care enough to say anything.

He wore one of those tight-fitting brown UPS uniforms.

He still looked melancholy, but in a different way. His eyes said, take a walk, asshole. I've seen men die. Men better than you.

I asked him why he left Tallahassee. He said fuck Tallahassee.

Hank's a lot easier to talk to these days. Oh, he goes by that now. Hank. Everyone calls him that. It's a good fit.

I meet Hank at the bar a couple times a week. He's got cash problems, so I cover both our drinks. Sometimes I talk, but most of the time I let him do all the talking. He updates me on his folks. Get a few more into him, he'll pull out his wallet and show me pictures of his two little girls. Precious. He's in a custody battle over the youngest.

When he gets in one of his moods, he'll go into some of what he saw over in the desert. It's the stuff of nightmares. I wouldn't want those memories trapped in my head. But he can talk about it so calm like. All the bloody little details— they don't even faze him. That's the creepiest part.

He doesn't use words like *weltschmerz* anymore. He could if he wanted to. I wouldn't mind. But he doesn't. He's not that kind of guy.

Keep the Ring

See, Martha has extra-sensory perception, but she's also a goddamn liar. Once, she said, don't go out tonight. There'll be sleet and snow everywhere. You'll swerve into a semi and die on impact.

So I stayed in. Watched TV on the sofa all night.

The next morning in bed I looked over at Martha and thought, 'godammit, it didn't even snow last night. She said all that garbage so I wouldn't go get tanked at the nudie bar.'

"No shit, Sherlock," said Martha, before I even got a word out.

Don't ever marry a mind reader.

Not ever.

Clark

I won't say we all do, but quite a number of vampires possess a modest collection of human friends. You wouldn't think that it would be worth the effort, but it's really quite essential toward maintaining equilibrium through difficult periods. One's existence is bound to eventually grow cumbersome when faced with eternity. Not everyone concentrates on it extensively, but speaking for myself personally, now and again I suffer moderately painful existential crises. Frequently, such crises come right after a meal: there I am, crouching over a fresh corpse, coppery blood dripping down my chin, my eyes glazed over and staring out into the void. I think, this is not me, this is not all that I am. I am not my insatiable blood-lust. This thirst, it is only one relic in an elaborate museum of characteristics. I am a being. I have a consciousness.

Clark was one of my human friends, until he died of cancer. I have enjoyed a large host of human friends, and I have watched them *all* die from one or another cause. Except for Clark, they have all asked me to help them become vampires.

It is simple enough to transform a human into a vampire, but it occurs rather infrequently. On the surface, it sounds lovely: surround yourself with undying confidants with whom to share immortality. Prost! But the unsweetened reality is that, by and large, I bear no deep desire for the company of vampires. A lot of them are insufferable, crass and disgustingly bourgeois. However, you can't blame an immortal being for putting on airs; outside of feeding and avoiding sunlight, we haven't any binding commitments; so naturally, over the course of a millennium, we'll fashion all appearances of high cultivation, that is, a warehouse of refined classical tastes.

But a rather boorish standoff usually proceeds whenever two vampires find themselves inhabiting the same environment.

As such, I'm never eager to convert a human into yet another undead elitist. In two thousand years, I've only done it twice, and sorely regret each instance. But my human friends, they always request it. We enjoy a pleasant, casual friendship until mortality taps upon their bedroom windowpane. Then, they suddenly morph into desperate, clinging toward whatever they think might keep them above the surface of existence. It is a flavorless subject that, frankly, spoils the taste of friendship. In the first place, I find myself somewhat put off by their ingratitude. That is to say, these creatures, they overlook the white elephant in the room: the very fact that I am predisposed to devour them at any moment, at any time, whenever and should I choose. Beside that, it's quite an intimate field to breach, and I am not comfortable discussing it on a whim. Allowing a human passage into infinity is the closest act that we vampires have to sexual intercourse, and we vampires are all, so to speak, abstinent creatures. Humans don't fully comprehend this, so I try to laugh away the topic, or gracefully skirt it. Ah, you would not wish to live forever, I'd say. Think of the worst fit of boredom you have ever experienced. I've spent whole decades in such a state. Or maybe I'd say, why would you wish to be a vampire? It is akin to a lifelong diet of condensed milk, condensed milk forever, condensed milk and nothing more.

Usually, I can find some way to elude it, at first at least, until they grow so desperate and irrational that I have no choice but to drop all emotional pretense and outright refuse them.

No. You may be my food and you may be my friend, but you shall never, never share my blood.

Clark was different, however. He never once asked for immortality. Not after he first learned of the cancer. Not when he learned that it was malignant. I was so baffled that I began to offer it to him, half-jokingly at first. I'd say, you needn't go through with this. I could see to it that the hairs stay atop that charming head of yours. He'd chuckle without responding. You're a peculiar fellow, I'd say, many humans would commit genocide for what I offer you.

He'd just shake his head, grinning.

Well yeah, he'd say, but then they'd just have to keep on killing forever, right? No thanks, sir.

When his health saw rapid decline, I found myself offering with increased urgency. Each time, he rejected my gift.

S'not for me, buddy boy, he'd say. Never wanted more than the guest room at this hotel, heh heh.

This is a facet of humanity that I cannot comprehend. Well, I can attest that immortality is all rot. Slumber, boredom and rot. By and large, the obstacles far outnumber the advantages. But an immortal being is a being, after all, and I cannot fathom a being that looks from infinity to oblivion, and ultimately chooses oblivion. A fear that seizes me whenever I dare to consider myself bearing that mortal declaration that one day, *I shall be no longer.* It wakes me every afternoon; it restrains me from stepping out into the naked daylight, thrusting my naked chest onto the point of a wooden stake.

I shall be no longer, I shall be no longer. If I were human, if I still existed as a finite beast, I would repeat this phrase every day, several times a day, until the phantom behind it dematerialized.

I sat beside his bed, held his hand during the last few moments of Clark's life, as he lay upon the hospital mattress. His mind and body were sustained by a network of plastic tubing and the liquid contents traveling therein. Even then, I whispered to him, it does not have to be this way, my dear. You do not have to end.

He did not respond. He simply ended.

The Biggest Something

I almost died yesterday. I was on my lunch break, walking
around the square with my headphones on. Then I crossed
the street and walked right in front of a bus. It would have
splattered me everywhere, but some dude came from out of
nowhere and pushed me out the way. The bus got him instead.
He made a crunching noise as he smacked against the street.
I hope I never hear that sound again.

It's crazy what that does to you. Almost dying. I think
everyone should almost die. You can't ever look at life the
same way again, not unless you force yourself to forget what
it was like to almost die. I don't really mean what it's like to
almost die, because at the time you don't know what the heck
is going on. But then afterward you realize that your whole
stupid universe was about to end. In one second, everything
you know and everyone you've seen and everything you have
and everything else is gone, all gone, gone for good. At
least for you. The universe is gone or you're gone—same
difference. If a tree falls and you don't hear it, either the tree
doesn't exist or you don't exist. Something doesn't exist.

The worst or best part of it is that right when you get
comfortable and you think, wow, I dodged a bullet, well then
it dawns on you that hey, wait, I dodged that *bullet,* but it only
means another bullet is going to get me. If you don't die one
way, you're going to die some other way. Something out there
has your number. Maybe now or maybe later. Definitely one
day. Time doesn't seem that long. A day is the same as ten
years.

I hate it. I shouldn't be twenty-three and feeling like this. I shouldn't be twenty-three and feeling like this. I shouldn't feel like this until like eighty-three, when I'm old and ugly and can't remember where I put my fake eye (I don't know why I picture myself having a fake eye when I'm old, but I do). That's when you're supposed to think about death all the time: when you're too old to have anything better to do.

But what's worse is, I found out that the man who saved my life was really rotten. I mean a total loser. He was this creepy black guy that went to jail a bunch of times. He was living in a halfway house even though he had like six or seven kids all over the city. Before he died, he was a bagger at a grocery store. He'd been convicted once for robbing a liquor store, once for assaulting a stripper at a strip club, once for drunk driving, and another for, well... he used to be a maintenance man at a grade school, and he got caught molesting a little boy in the gym locker room.

Now, he's dead. Dead and dead and dead. He won't touch no more boys and he won't knock-up no more girls. He won't bag no more groceries and he won't save no one else's life. He's done. That's it.

I wish I had never found out anything about him. If I could, I would change everything about him in my mind. Well, he would still be black, but he wouldn't be so creepy. He would be my protector, my superhero (and I don't mean a drunken psycho superhero, I mean a *real* hero). He would take care of me, in the dark. Every time I felt bad, I could just think of him watching over me, ready to swoop down whenever I needed him.

Or maybe he was a younger-looking dude that was crazy in love with me, always watching from a distance but too nervous to talk to me, until he finally saw his chance to make the biggest sacrifice that anyone could ever make. I even imagined that he carried my picture in a locket, or in his wallet, but I couldn't come up with a way for that to *not* make him creepy again, so I nixed it. No picture. He would just have to walk that thin line between guardian angel and stalker.

He wasn't really any of those things. Not a guardian angel or a stalker. Even a psycho stalker would've been cooler than what he was. He was just a crusty dude on welfare with seven kids who probably all hated him and were glad that he was dead. Probably, the only nice thing he ever did was push me away from that bus. I just don't know why he even bothered doing that. He was such a rotten man.

But now… now I'm thinking about doing something. Something big. Quitting my job at the comic store. Getting a job where I have to cover up my tattoos and stop dying my hair. Maybe go back to school. Meet somebody nice, save up money for a house and start making babies. I don't know. Okay that might all be a bunch of crap. That sounds really lame and even typing it makes me feel slightly lamer than I was before. But I need to do something. I mean, I'm cool with working at the comic store, but it won't last forever. Old Harry is going to die one day, and when he does, the store will close down. I'll have to find a new job. By then, I'll be forty and all the jobs will be going to the little whipper snappers. I'll be this tired old biddy still living at my auntie's apartment. And then one day my auntie's going to die and I'll be homeless. I'll have to sell hobo newspapers on the street every day.

That'll be so sad because I'll be this crummy hag that doesn't know diddly squat except comic books and video games. And even that will suck because nobody wants to talk about comic books and video games with crummy old hags. I'll just take up space and right before I drop dead, I'll be like, what a copout, the shiftiest dude on the planet saved my life and all I got out was this lousy T-shirt.

I don't even know if he saved me on purpose. Maybe he didn't mean to. Maybe he was gonna grab me and drag me into a dark alley to rape me up the butt. I don't know and I never will. It's not fair.

I want to believe that he saw me about to get hit and he thought, let me do one good deed to make up for my whole stupid, miserable life.

I can't imagine anybody thinking that way though.

I have a picture of him. It's a mug shot. My best friend Marius' uncle is a cop. He talked to the right people and got a photocopy of it for me. I don't think he was supposed to, but everyone has been extra nice to me lately. Like, they're all apologizing that the gross town troll saved my life when no one else could. I scanned the photocopy and printed it out as a wallet size pic on glossy paper, and put it in a little silver frame. It's kind of fuzzy but whatever, no one sees it but me. I keep it under my bed. I hate that I have it and sometimes I hate him, but I will probably always keep the picture, until I die. Then, after I die, somebody will find the picture and won't have a clue. No one will know that my hero was awful and that I hated him and that I hated how I kept his picture my whole life and wouldn't let myself get rid of it.

Every morning, I wake up, get out of bed, and take the picture out from under the mattress. I look at it. The first thing I force myself to think is, I'm no better than this man. He's dead. One day, I'll be dead too. Every dead body is no different than every other dead body. Maybe, he's even better than me; he only did one good thing in his entire life--but that one good thing might be bigger than anything I ever do.

The next thing I think is, today, I'm going to do something really nice for a stranger. Someone at the store will be short on change and I'll say that's okay, I got you. Or I'll get up from my bus seat when an old lady wants to sit down, or at the diner I'll make sure not to stiff the waitress on the tip, even when I only drink coffee all night. But those aren't really big things. I want to do something really big. One day I will. Maybe right after I finish writing this. Or tomorrow. Probably tomorrow. If not tomorrow then definitely one

The Problem With Genius

Buddy loves him some aliens. He reads books about extraterrestrials, watches TV specials on UFO sightings. He wears shirts with those aliens that have thin, silver bodies, bobble heads, and black eyes. He really believes in aliens. We always argue about it.

I usually say, even if aliens existed, I couldn't see how they were smart enough to build spaceships and travel light years, but so dumb that they had nothing better to do than peep around on the worst planet in the galaxy.

Buddy says they're studying Earth to prepare for mass invasion, but I think that's silly too. If I were a super-smart alien, I wouldn't bother invading a cruddy planet already three-fourths ruined by pollution. I'd find a healthy planet.

But Buddy thinks I'm confusing aliens with gods. Gods are ideas and aliens are things, he says. He says, look at me. I can tell you everything about quantum physics and nuclear engineering. I love coding; if I wanted to, I could probably hack into a commercial bank and wipe out dozen of accounts before anyone noticed. But here I am, thirty-three and living out of my mom's basement, sleeping on the same ratty futon I had when I was twelve.

So then if aliens are such smart dummies, I say, why even care? There are way more interesting creatures out there. Like whales, what the hell is with them? Meh, said Buddy. All whales do is swim.

That got me wondering. I pictured sperm whales, deep in the ocean, thinking, 'Boy, humans are idiots. They can build spaceships and fly in outer space, but instead of doing that all the time, they just walk, walk, walk, everyday walking, walking for no reason.'

Exit

There's a quarry about eight miles south on the expressway and that's where I'll do it. If I can't get to it by car, I'll park on the shoulder and reach it by foot. It would be easier with the car, but they don't make it easy anymore. These days, seems like everyone's looking for a good, deep quarry to dive into, just to see what happens, see if it'll heal everything once and for all. Even people who don't really want to close the book, even them, they take a look at the quarry as they drive on by and they think, why the hell not? But then they keep on going. Nobody knows how to answer that, not for sure, and so there's probably a wire fence lined down the length of the quarry side. Can't drive through it. Climbing, no problem.

I'm not going to do it though. Yes I am. First I'm going to get some breakfast. Breakfast for lunch. It's one sixteen and by a quarter to three, give or take, I'll splat myself all around the bottom of the quarry. A Rounda Clock serves breakfast food any time of the day. It's always morning somewhere, so we'll always have breakfast here! That's their motto. On the menu. It's cute.

As soon as I sit in the booth, I don't want breakfast anymore. Or lunch. Or dinner. All I want is a cup of coffee with no sugar. I like my coffee how I like my women: lukewarm, bitter and heartless. I want to stare hard into the mug and wait for magical letters to swim up to the depths and tell me what to do.

My car is a Thunderbird and it is a piece of junk. I named it Alabama. I've never been to Alabama.

The diner is very bright. But it's all natural light; the sun burns so bright through the windows that everything shimmers, so that you can see the dirt everywhere but you can also see what shines underneath the dirt. Everything in A Rounda Clock looks dirtier and greasier than it has a right to be but you can't complain in a place like this, because it's still shining under the dirt, somewhere, and anyway it's awfully silly to criticize a greasy spoon diner for being greasy.

I wake up every morning and every morning I think of a million reasons to live and then think of reasons not to live. Slowly I started noticing that the reasons to live weren't reasons at all but excuses.

Most of the other people at the diner look like truckers. All men. Good ol' boys. Flannel and beards and jeans and scruffy boots everywhere, but all in the dirty working man way, not like an indie kid thing. It's far into the afternoon but it might as well be the crack of dawn. Everyone looks tired. So tired. It's fairly quiet. Everyone I peek at, the look on everyone's face, almost everyone, seems to say hey, man, don't fucking talk to me. I understand that look. Thinking like that. Sometimes I can't figure out people that don't look that way. What's their secret? I don't know.

I won't do it. Not if the waitress is beautiful. She'll be beautiful and we'll lock eyes and she'll figure everything out, just from looking into my eyes, and then, well, then I won't have to do it anymore. Then, I'll be okay.

The waitress is not beautiful. She's tired and mean looking. Her blonde hair isn't very blonde anymore. Her skin is permanently sunburned.

It looks like life elbowed her in the face about a hundred times.

She pours the coffee. Do I want anything to eat? No. I do not.

The plan was to order a real big meal. Pancakes and waffles and sausage and bacon and buttered grits and scrambled eggs and hash browns and rye toast and white toast and French toast and plenty of maple syrup over everything. The waitress would come out with a few plates, and when I cleared off those plates she would bring out a few more plates. I would get full really early and then keep on eating, and eating, right up until I was almost about to throw up. Then I would pay the bill, leave my wallet for the tip, and drive over to the quarry. That was the plan.

Staring into the coffee. Magic letters didn't swim up to the surface.

I should at least have a cigarette to go with it.

I don't smoke.

The waitress is not beautiful, but if she looks at me, if she still looks at me, and figures it out, then I won't do it. No. She doesn't have to figure it out. If she looks at me and asks, what's wrong, honey? If she asks that, then I won't do it. That's kind of like figuring it out. Nobody ever asks me what's wrong. She doesn't have to be a mind reader. All she has to do is care.

Yeah, I've also got a fifth of scotch in the trunk.

I didn't think I was going to have to use it but now that my
stomach feels this way I think that I might need it. I'm a
lightweight, and so I won't need to drink much but I will
drink it all down anyway, because what the heck, I don't
have to worry about a hangover.

Sitting there, staring into my coffee with my hands wrapped
around the coffee mug: I'm anxious, like I'm about to go get
behind a podium to speak in front of a thousand people. Only
I haven't memorized my speech, I haven't even prepared one
yet. When you feel like that, something starts to tingle right in
the center of your chest and move up to your throat for a while
and then spreads to the back of your head. Then it stays there,
it stays everywhere. And you're ashamed of it and you don't
want anyone to look at you because you feel like they can see
it on you, all over you, sweating out of your pores.

The waitress comes back to my booth and she asks me, need
a warm up? I shake my head. I do not need a warm up.
The mug is half full and I do not need a warm up.

I look around. If it will not be the waitress, then maybe it will
be someone else. She will open the door and walk in at just
the right moment. She will also be planning to drive to the
quarry, after her last meal. She will sit alone at a booth. She
will lose her appetite and order the coffee. She will stare into
the mug for a long time, looking for an answer. Any answer.

Magic letters will swim up to the surface and say, LOOK UP.
She will look up and see me, sitting across from her. We
will recognize each other and once we do, we won't need
the quarry anymore. The spell will be broken. And then
everything else will happen the way it is supposed to happen.

There is a song playing on the radio. The radio is near the front counter. I don't recognize the song. Maybe there is no song and I am only willing a song into the restaurant, willing it to play softly, and I prefer it to be a song I do not know. Whether I will it to be or not I can almost hear it and it is the song you would expect to hear at a diner in the afternoon, a decent enough song that nobody ever gets excited over.

It's two-fifteen. It's two-fifteen and I should start heading over to the quarry.

Magic letters do not swim up to the surface.

I fish the wallet out of my pants pocket, set it on the table. I finish off the rest of the coffee, get up from the booth. I'm going to need the scotch. I'm going to need the scotch just to give myself the courage to start the car. I wish I smoked because cigarettes are supposed to be almost as good with liquor as they are with coffee.

I head for the front door. Maybe she will open the door from the outside just as I reach for the knob from the inside. She will. She is about to get lunch at her favorite diner at her usual time of day, and she will turn the knob just as I reach for it. Our eyes will meet and we will say, with our eyes, right then, *Finally. There you are.*

I reach for the knob. I turn it. I open the door. I walk out of the diner.

I'm fishing around the trunk when the waitress comes running out of the diner, running after me, waiving my wallet in the air. I shut the trunk.

I thought I was too late, says the waitress, and she says it perfectly, just like in movies. And I'm supposed to give her a knowing grin, nod and say, *so did I.* Or maybe I should say, *me too.* Or, I thought so, too. No. I'm supposed to take the wallet, and caress her fingers at the same time, and say, *it's never too late.* I would say that. *It's never too late.* Then she will understand everything.

The Greater Good

There's a giant robot tearing up the Loop, tearing it to bits,
but to be perfectly honest with you I'd rather not tell Amazing
Man, if it's all the same. He's been on a binge, another one
of his binges, for the last forty hours, and it's really best for
everyone if he just stays in his apartment until he floats down
from Cloud Number Nine. The robot's going to keep right on
smashing cars and batting pedestrians with broken lamp posts.
And that's a bad thing. No arguing that. I just don't know if
the solution is getting Amazing Man tangled up into the mess.
Even while sober he's iffy, and when he's hopped up on fairy
dust he tends to go light on the *hero* half of *superhero*. That's
putting it mildly. One time, after magic mushrooms and a fifth
of gin, he tried to 'catch' fleeing bank robbers by picking up a
station wagon and throwing it at them. Let me be crystal clear:
the robbers were fleeing *by foot,* and Amazing Man tried to
stop them by hurling a station wagon at them. The worst of it
is that it cleared the bank robbers by a long shot and crashed
into a flower shop.

Everybody on the street stopped and stared. I mean everybody;
the pedestrians, the robbers, me. Even Amazing Man's eyes
went real wide, like, oh crap, was that me, did I do that? The
only funny part—and it wasn't funny until a while later—
was that after about a minute of total silence on the street, the
robbers dropped the money, threw up their hands and shouted,
"Holy fuck! You win!" The bottom line was that Amazing
Man had caused millions of dollars in property damage--and
one fatality--to catch thieves who had stolen approximately
two hundred thousand dollars in *marked* bills.

And so I say: let the robot have his fill. The insurance industry still hasn't figured out how to deal with this stuff, so they haven't yet found a way to define giant robot monsters and super-villain machinations as catastrophic events. As a result, just about everything worthwhile in this town is insured out the derriere. Outside of that, the only real problem is staying out of the robot's way—which most *sensible* civilians should be able to do, on account of, you can hear the robot coming from a mile away. It doesn't take a brain surgeon to think hey, maybe I shouldn't take Lower Wacker Drive today. By the looks of it, a humungous, walking machine of destruction is right around there, pulverizing everything within reach. Maybe, just this once, I'll go off the beaten path to get to work.

I'd do something myself, but, well, I'm only good in support. Don't let the title Mega Boy fool you, I'm neither mega nor a boy, and definitely not both of those things combined. I don't have super powers, I turn forty-seven next month, and I haven't hit the gym in at least eleven years. What I have is a goofy looking green and yellow spandex costume, and Amazing Man's personal cell phone number. I try to use both as sparingly as possible, but you know how that goes. Really, my name should be Mega Bitch, because that's all I am, his little bitch: I buy his groceries, nurse him through hangovers and make him 'disappear' whenever someone tries to serve him up a summons. It's a thankless job. I'd have quit long ago, but he keeps throwing my promise back in my face. That's his real super power, if you ask me: guilt-tripping. So five years ago, he saved my wife from being eaten alive, when she fell into the shark tank at the Shedd Aquarium. Then here comes big stupid me pledging lifelong allegiance to the Ace of Schmucks.

But back then, I didn't know he was a screw off and a user, I just thought, well—come on, I grew up reading comic books, like everybody else.

I'll spare you the full story, but the punch line is that my wife has long since left me. To quote the letter: *I love Felix Mendelstein, but I have no respect for Mega Boy. Mega Boy is an insane person. I will not stay married to an insane person. I can not and will not, not for another minute, because it would make me even more of an insane person. I'm sorry, Felix.*

The police are going to have to tough it out this time. They all want me to contact the mighty hero. I turned off my phone long ago; by now my voice mail is probably full, with a good hundred or so text messages to boot. And while the evil robot lays waste to the city, our mighty hero is most likely whiling the hours on his living room floor, picking at the carpet. I say, the city's all the better for it.

Blush & Mumble

I used to hate hugs. I thought they were phony and stupid.
You grab hold of somebody, press them against your chest,
and squeeze. That's supposed to be a show of affection. Ha.
I never wanted to hug anyone and I didn't like being hugged.
I'd have rather shaken someone's hand, even though that's
stupid too. I read that handshaking started because white men
had to prove to each other that they weren't secretly holding
weapons. That's why handshaking never became as popular
with women, because we're supposed to be harmless no
matter what. It's all stupid when I think about it. But hugging
was definitely the dumbest. It's... it's like trying to be as close
as possible to someone, even though that person's mind is a
million miles away from yours. But gee, hey, we're hugging,
great, you must be special to me, this really means something,
this hugging business, we're practically the same person,
being so close like this, I can't tell me from you. Yeah, right.
So dumb.

That all changed after this one thing happened. Let me
explain.

I used to see this white girl all around the city. I thought she
was gorgeous. So sad and beautiful. I guess most people
would have thought she was kind of nerdy looking. She was
short, a little round. Somewhere in her early twenties, I'd say.
Fair skin, curly black hair. She always wore black, and I'd
counted three piercings on her face, although I missed a few
on her ears. Some people think that's a tough look, but it's not.
You can still see the nerd underneath that. No one can hide the
inner nerd. I can tell, anyway. You can always spot one of
your own.

I would see her on the trains and buses and stuff. She was always reading. I'd wonder, what's she reading now? And I'd try to peek and see what book it was. It was always something that I'd never heard of.

I wanted to say something to her, but I'm shy. Around new people, at least. Until I know what to make of them. And, come on, so many people in this city are so flipping crazy, it's easy to shut everybody out. When strangers come up to me I usually think, uh-oh, another one escaped from the looney bin. Either that, or else it'll be some smelly bum asking for money. I don't look like a bum and I hope I don't look like a crazy, but who's to say? Crazies don't think they're crazy. Maybe to everyone else I look like a raving basket case. And plus, nothing could ever have happened, not in a million years. She probably didn't even like women. Or maybe she was weird about dating a black woman, and had all these messed up ideas about black people that would just break my heart. If I'd even opened my big mouth, it all would have gone downhill. Then I'd have had to avoid her all the time because even making eye contact for two seconds would have been totally awkward. She'd have thought I was a stalker.

But even still I thought, hey, we can be friends. Friendship is so much cooler anyhow. To be honest, I don't really like dating. It's uncomfortable and weird and gives me migraines from getting so worked up and nervous. I don't mean headaches, I mean full blown, exploding, incapacitating migraines, where I get dizzy and feel like vomiting. I'm a total mess. The few times that I've even bothered dating were complete disasters.

I was super quiet each time, both 'cause I was nervous and couldn't think of anything cool to say, and because it felt like my brain was trying to bang it's way right out of my skull. On a couple of the dates, the girls sensed that something was wrong, but when they asked me if I was okay I just mumbled out some gibberish that might not have even sounded like English. And so, every girl I dated eventually thought I was either an idiot, boring, or bored. Sometimes they were right about those last two, but usually it was just 'cause I made myself sick wanting so badly to be perfect, so that no one would want to go away and disappear completely.

That's the worst part, cause even when not I'm interested in someone, I still think about her a lot. How she looked. The stuff she liked. The way she pronounced words differently, depending on where she was from. Where she put her hands while she talked. If she had good teeth or bad teeth or teeth that were crooked but somehow made her look more attractive. I think about that stuff over and over and it make me sad to think that I may not see any of it again. That whole person and everything along with her is gone forever, leaving behind a bunch of stupid memories that float around in my head until I start going bonkers. I hate that. But it happens all the time.

It's not just ladies, either. I'm that way about everybody. There's the balding subway conductor with the neat grey beard, who always sticks his head out of the conductor's car to smile at me and says good morning, my dear, with a thick Eastern European accent. There's the fresh out-of-college working girl with flaming blond hair and airbrushed skin and the white open-toed heels. She walks like a Woman With a Purpose. Her shoes pop against the platform like tiny fire crackers.

47

There's the Octopus Lady. I always seem to sit behind her on the train, and the back of her head looks like a hairy brown octopus sitting on top of a trench coat. Don't ask me why that's the image that comes to mind, but it does, every time. Then there's the older Asian man that looks like a turtle wearing a toupee. He has a huge hairy mole on his chin. He's always asleep on the train and probably misses his stop every day.

I know all of these people, even though I don't know any of them. Still, I want to keep them in my world. Of course, plenty of them have disappeared over the years but I still remember most of them. There are a lot.

Maybe she would have been another one of those vanishing people. She would have moved away and I would have kept on thinking about her, making up answers to various questions like, what's her favorite food? Is she dating anyone? Or is she like me, and thinks dating is stupid? Does she hate hugging people too? Wouldn't it be cool if her idea of a fun date is to stay home, eat pizza and chocolate gelato and watch old kung-fu movies? I wouldn't have to worry about kissing, or 'does she just think we're friends?' or anything like that, because screw that, whoa, Sonny Chiba just ripped out that guy's throat! Awesome! Or wait, maybe during, or no, right after something cool just happened in the movie, she would lean over and kiss me. On the cheek or on the lips. I wouldn't even see it coming, then—bam, there it was, right out there, and I wouldn't have to say anything. I wouldn't even have time to get nervous about it.

But heck, maybe she had a boyfriend. She probably did. He probably wore ripped jeans and metal band T-shirts.

And also a drummer. Definitely a drummer in some band.
A rock band, not a metal band, because it gives you that
extra edge when your shirt says that you listen to music
way more intense than the music you play. And the two of
them had matching lip rings; his-and-her lip rings. Maybe
even matching tattoos. Matching grim reaper tattoos,
because they're so bad, their love is death.

That would have been okay too. She'd still need a friend. You
can be in a relationship and still be even lonelier than if you
were single. Maybe her boyfriend spent all his time with the
band. Even when he wasn't with the band, all he did was talk
about the band, whether she was paying attention or not. Or
maybe they fought like crazy every other day, and whenever
she wanted quality time he'd say that she was suffocating him.
So then, she could call me up, in tears, after fighting with her
l'il drummer boy, and I could be the one to calm her down.
Or she could call me because he did something strange and
she wanted someone else's diagnosis. You know, does that
mean he's just not that into me, or is he about to propose? Or
hold on, wait, he always went off on business trips to different
states. No, not business trips. He's not a business trip guy.
He's too young, too *damn the man* for that. There was the
band. He was always touring. Always on the road. The cool
part was, while he was gone, I was the first person she'd want
to call. Just to chat. Nothing special, just chatting—about
anything. Or she'd come over and we'd watch kung-fu movies
and talk. Sometimes we'd have deep conversations, politics
and life, and sometimes we'd get goofy and ask each other,
what if every Senator had to fight a ninja to prove that he was
strong enough to join the Senate? Oh, and not just any ninja—
Sho Kosugi.

But not just Sho Kosugi—Sho Kosugi from the seventies.
I think a strong politician might be able to take down the
present-day Sho Kosugi. He's pretty old now. But back then?
Sho nuff butt-kicker!

Or no, hold the phone, she didn't have a boyfriend (sorry, I'm
all over the place!), but she wanted one. And so she'd call
me up all the time, and sometimes even in the middle of the
night, feeling bad about not having a boyfriend, how much
she wanted one. A lot of people would get ticked-off after a
while. They would be like, darn it, girl, shut that man-lovin'
mouth of yours. But I wouldn't mind at all. Really, I'd be
happy that, out of everybody in the whole world, she chose
me. I was the one she needed to call in the middle of the night.
I'd stay awake and keep quiet and listen, because that's what
she'd want. It would kill me to think of how unhappy she'd be
if she didn't have anyone to call up, especially on those late,
late nights, when you can't sleep and it feels like there's no
one else in the whole world. She'd feel like she didn't even
exist, that no one did. But no, there'd be me. I'd be there. It
would be like that one poem, what's the one, about being like
someone's air, invisible and necessary.

I saw her around the city for almost a full year. It's not even
like we seemed to have the same schedule, because I would
see her at different times during the day, in different parts of
the city. At first it was just, hmph, she looks interesting. Then
I saw her more often. In the last few months I was all, hey, I
should say something. By then, she definitely recognized me
too. When we would pass one another on the street, we would
give each other the 'hey, you' look. You know what I'm
talking about. It's different from a lot of the other looks
that strangers give each other. often though.

There are a lot of looks. There's the look where you're kind of smiling, but not really; that's for when you want to politely acknowledge someone but you don't want them to think that you have any interest in talking to them. It's more stretching your lips than smiling. Then there's the slimy sleazoid smile; no real need to describe that one. Then there's the really friendly one, the good one, the one that says 'I would love to talk to you if I had a reason to, but I don't have a reason, so I'll just put the whole friendship into this one smile.' I love that smile, it's really great. It doesn't come very I don't give many people that smile because I'm afraid they'll think it's my sleazoid smile. I hope I don't have a sleazoid smile. Actually I frown most of the time. Maybe too much. Especially since I moved into the city. It's my 'don't talk to me, you don't even have anything important to say' frown.

By the end of that year, I was pretty sure I was going to make a go for it. Go up and talk to her. I really looked forward to the rare occasions that I saw her, where we'd share eye contact, a silent hello. I wanted to say something like, Hey. I have to know. What's your name? Like that. Something pleasant and safe. And harmless.

I saw her at the subway one morning. That's when I convinced myself to do it. I would wait until we faced each other. Or I'd just march right up and tap her on the shoulder. One of the two. Then I'd go into my whole spiel, and we'd become friends. Acquaintances. But it'd be natural and comfortable and good. It had to be comfortable. Otherwise, she might change her daily schedule, and I'd never see her again. Or she'd move to another state. Or anything.

We stood at opposite ends of the platform, waiting on the train. I don't think she saw me. I was starting to get jittery. I wouldn't do it. I would. I wouldn't.

I heard the train approaching. Okay, now. Do it. Before she's gone forever. Stop huffin' and puffin.' Do it already. Don't think about how you're blushing the shade of a tomato. I slowly shuffled over to her, hoping she'd catch sight of me and I wouldn't have to tap her on the shoulder or anything. Touching her might weird her out.

I was about five feet away from her when she took a step toward the tracks and then two more steps and then hopped off the edge of the platform.

I remember the blood and the screaming. So much blood. So much screaming. Then everything went mute, like plunging underwater. I backed against the wall, slid to the ground and blacked out. I might not have blacked out. Maybe. Maybe not. I don't like thinking about it.

I do remember that suddenly, the bearded train conductor was there. He was staring down at me. Then, he was holding me. I didn't fight. I thought, if my grandfather was still alive, he would hold me like this. Someone handed him a towel. He wrapped it around my shoulders and led me out of the sub-way. He took my right hand and pumped it, then whispered something into my ears with this thick accent. I don't know what he said, I only heard the sounds. He rode with me in the ambulance, close by, holding my hand. He stayed with me the whole day at the hospital.

His name is Havel. He has a niece four years older than me. We meet for coffee and bagels in the morning once a month, every month—on the same day, that day.

When we meet, before we sit down he gives me a tight, warm bear hug. It's my favorite part of the morning, or heck, it's my favorite thing period. He says so much with that hug. I'm glad that you are alive, he says. I'm so glad that you did not die, that I can feel how alive you are. You exist. This is true. I can feel it here, right here, against my own chest. I try to say the same, when I hug him back.

He says that he is only a train conductor in disguise, just in the U.S., and that in Europe he's a famous poet and philosopher. I don't know about that. He seems to exaggerate sometimes. But it's cool, I like it. Everything is big and grandiose with him. He makes lots of dramatic gestures with his hands. Clasping them together, waving, opening his arms out wide when he wants to talk about the whole country, the world, the universe. Even if he is telling all lies, well, they're enjoyable lies.

Havel says that I should learn Czech, even though I'm black and Cherokee and not even a little bit Czech. But Havel says, you must learn! For me. My niece, she will never learn. Hannah, she is my joy. My precious jewel. But speaking in the language of her family? She is no good for this. Or she will make no effort. I can not say. But you, my dear, you were born to speak Czech! This is no lie.

I don't know. I don't know if I could learn another language. I always thought that if I ever tried to learn a language, it would be Polish. Or I'd go off to a reservation and try to learn the Cherokee language. But Czech? That's tough.

Well, it would be nice if we could meet for coffee and bagels and only speak in Czech. And he would tell me about when he lived in Prague, or how beautiful it is, and how he wants to see it once more before he dies. And then, maybe, he would become a little quiet, be cause he'd just brought up death. After a few minutes of staring down at his coffee quietly, he would ask me if I still think about her. I'd say yes, every single day. He would nod and say yes. It is the same with me. Every day. It must be like this. I forget, I do not know what she looks like now. In my mind, she looks like my niece. Just like this. But she is more exciting than my niece shall ever be. I love my niece, love her dearly. She is very precious to me. He would smile. A warm hug, in the smile. But you know, of course you do. How I mean this.

Sheldon; False Idolatry

I wish I was like Amazing Man. He can stop bullets and
punch through steel. I buy his comics and clip out his
newspaper stories. Sometimes in my room I wear my
blanket as a cape and fight make-believe baddies.

If I was Amazing Man I'd pulverize my step-dad Jared. He's
always drunk and slapping me and mom around. He says,
"Whenever you want to take me on, little man, just try. You
even get the first lick." If I had super powers, I'd knock him
from here to Toledo. Then he'd be sorry.

It'll never happen but that's okay.

Our Heroes

I bartend at Binky's, this bar over on the south side. Here and there, Amazing Man shows up to get himself pissed on whiskey sours. Y'know, big, super Amazing Man. Strong as thirty oxes, can take bullets to the chest'n laugh. Always on the news about this'n that. In person he's a real nipple, he is. All's he does is piss and moan, all night.

"Whole world's bunk," he'll whine. "'Help,' they say, 'stop the supervillains!' But kill them? 'Oh nooooooo, only supervillains can kill.' S'bass akwards."

Around closing time, he'll shout "Whoosh!" and pretend to fly away. Then he'll giggle'n crawl on home. Flying ain't one a' his super powers.

I'll admit, the bastard can hold his liquor alright.

But I bet they all can.

Off Road With Casper

I hadn't seen Casper in a decade. Yet there he was, in the flesh
& not one of those ten years had grazed him.

I take the subway El home from work, late in the afternoon.
It's a 5, 6 block walk, then down the stairs and underground,
State & Jackson. That's where I found him: in the subway,
sitting Indian style against the wall next to a presumably
broken payphone. His head was a mushroom of brown black,
with a smooth face that never came near a 5 o'clock shadow.
No shoes, no socks. A country boy with a banjo. He named the
banjo Ol' Gunner. His grandfather gave it to him when he was
6 & 6 he remained. He sang as if he needed everyone to hear
him, no matter what kind of damage it did to his vocal chords.

I thought it would be one of those uncomfortable meetings
where he wouldn't recognize me but I would recognize that
the years had turned him into a batshit crazy person.

As I approached, he continued strumming his banjo &
strangling the air out of his lungs, his eyes smashed shut.
Then, finally, he finished. I tossed a few bucks into the open
guitar case. He peeked down at the bills, up at me, then
smiled through his eyes & shouted Jonas!

I phoned Chelsea & told her not to wait on me for dinner &
that we'd have a guest sleeping over for the night. She was
exasperated; I assured her, it wasn't an issue, she'd already
be in bed by the time we got in. We wouldn't interrupt her
low-key weeknight.

Casper was just wandering the states for a bit; he was only in one particular town for the short term. I'd take him out for dinner & let him crash on the couch. His train left the next morning, the Southwest Chief to Saint Louis, then Kansas City & Denver & straight on through to California. If he went in that order.

In college, we hit a lot of parties & basement shows, scoring cheap beer & weed & waking up on couches. We played in a shitty hardcore band with our friend Big Tobacco & occasionally Casper's cousin Ramona. We got into a bunch of wild shit that somehow never managed to get us arrested or in the hospital. Win.

It's sad & amusing how stupid we were. Saying fuck it all & building up our own community, our own insulated crappy world.

These days, around the north side where I live, I see all these new punks, with their dyed hair & thrift store clothes. Coffee breath & bummed cigarettes. They don't belong anywhere, not anywhere in the world, so they camp out around those dumpsters with all the other kids that don't belong anywhere, squatting & drinking or staring & not giving a shit. They all want to die & secretly think they'll live forever.

We took a taxi to this fusion place where the portions are tiny & the bill is not. The waitresses were porcelain, swathed in black & fashionably unimpressed. I had eaten there 2 or 3 times, for work lunches; I thought it might be nice to treat Casper to a fancy meal. As soon as we sat down & I read his face, I knew I'd made a huge mistake.

I ordered the duck & he ordered the cheapest dish on the menu. He only picked at his food. Halfway through the meal, he reminded me that he was vegan. The only things he could eat on the menu were the couscous & the steamed vegetables. He didn't want either.

The Casper I remember would have yelled at me for bringing him to such a place. This new Casper, however, only sat & picked at his food & let the FUCK YOU hang in the air. I tried to fight through the discomfort & asked him about life.

Sometimes, Casper toured with a few hardcore bands. He'd either open for them, help them transport sound equipment or help them sell merchandise after the shows. He'd done shows on his own, but it didn't really appeal to him. He worked at a few homeless shelters, did some bartending, a few other things. He was accepted into the Peace Corps, but he turned them down at the last minute, calling the whole thing all a bogus popularity contest. Oh & he'd traveled all over the world. The drunkest he'd ever been was in Brussels. Zimbabwe had the worst poverty he'd ever seen. He could speak a little German, a little French, a little Russian, some Czech & a little Mandarin Chinese. A couple others, here & there. Also, he used to stay with some punks in Romania. Pretty soon, he was going to make it back over there & hang out for a while.

Casper asked me if I'd done any traveling. Instead of mentioning the trip Chelsea & I took to Cancun, I shook my head & said nope, not really. Then to dress it up I said that one of these days, we might take a trip to Paris. He looked really confused & said who's we, you & me? I apologized & said no, we means Chelsea & I.

That's the thing with marriage, I said, you suddenly stop speaking in the 1st person.

I've used that joke before, several times in the past; it usually gets a laugh or a chuckle—at least a smile. But Casper got really serious & said that's no good, it shouldn't be that way. I said I was joking, even though I really wasn't.

I said, we might plan a trip to Paris. Maybe next summer, or the summer after, who knows. Casper said no, not who knows. You need to go. As soon as you can. It's not like you don't have the money, he said. I told him that it wasn't so easy. We had to plan it all out, budget everything, save up a good chunk of vacation time. Casper shook his head.

Man, he said, I lived in Leipzig for a while. I'll tell you how I got there. I bused tables at a diner until I had enough for the plane ticket. For 3 months, I lived out of my cousin Ramona's walk-in closet. For 4 months after that, my friend Buddy let me stay in his mom's garage & I had to hide out cause he didn't want his ma to find out.

When I had enough cash, he said, I bought a 1-way ticket & took off the same day. You? You could buy a round-trip ticket right now if you wanted to. You'd probably still have lots of money left over. No kidding, I could help you pack & we could go to the airport right now. Anywhere you want to go. Anywhere.

I didn't answer him, so that it would seem like I thought he was only speaking hypothetically. He wasn't. He was dead serious & I knew it.

But I also knew that I wasn't going anywhere except to the train station in the morning, to drop him off before work.

I didn't really want him on the couch getting it all stanky, but I took a pass on that one. I said hey, if you want you can hit the shower as long as you don't walk around naked afterwards. Chelsea wouldn't be into that. But Casper shook his head & said thanks, but I'm so dang tired, I'm just gonna crash.

Only he didn't seem tired & we stayed up another 2 hours in the living room. He glanced around, then honed in on the bookshelf & quietly scanned over the books. After silently examining each 1, he went over & withdrew 4 books, setting them aside on the couch. Then he leafed through the books 1 by 1. Only after all that did he ask me if he could borrow the books. Obviously loaning him the books meant letting him have them, cause he'd never given them back. But I'd owned the books for over a decade. One of them, I hadn't finished; 2 others, I hadn't even started. The last one, I used to worship. I'd read it 6 times. In college, I carried it around with me everywhere I went. Whenever I became depressed, I'd read a few random pages to cheer myself up. When I was serious about any girl I dated, I lent her the book to read. I even broke up with a few girls because they either didn't bother to read it or didn't like it.

Then I married Chelsea. Chelsea didn't give a good goddamn about the book. Somehow, I was okay with that. We bought a condo together & a bookshelf to decorate the condo. My book became another book decorating a bookshelf decorating a condo.

Take them, I said. All 4. They're yours. Casper mumbled
something quickly about how he'd find a way to mail back
the books after he finished them. However, he didn't have my
address & never asked for it. Most likely, once he finished the
books, he'd give them away, throw them away or toss them
somewhere & forget about them.

At one point I said it's late, I better cash in. His train wasn't
until 10, but I get up way earlier than that to get ready for
work. I'd have to drop him off at the station early & he could
just hang tight until departure. He said, no problem, his voice
almost at a whisper, eyes fastened to the book.

Before I left Casper, he was picking up Ol' Gunner, getting
ready to start playing. I stopped him short & said, that's not
such a good idea. Even if I didn't mind it, Chelsea would have
a fit & I'd hear about it forever. If you want, you can watch
some TV.

No way, said Casper.

He'd stopped watching television years ago. It made him feel
anxious. He said, TV & movies just fool you into thinking
you've lived more life than you really have.

He went on & on. I didn't really want to hear it. I acted like
I agreed with him. But then he said oh yeah, you agree with
me? Then what's this big ol' television doing right smack in
the middle of the room?

I said well, after working 10 hours a day, sometimes I just
wanna come home, sit on the couch & shut off my brain for a
while.

That's stupid, he said, that doesn't make sense. Why would you want to shut off your brain? Shutting your brain off is like being dead. Isn't it? After working all day, why would you want to be dead all night? That's fucking dumb.

I couldn't explain it to him & I didn't want to.

I said, I don't know. That's just how it is sometimes. Good night.

Somehow I slept through the singing. I might have slept right on through it 'til morning, but Chelsea jerked upright from her pillow & shouted WHAT THE FUCK?!?

Which I did hear. Loud & clear.

Immediately following, I heard the strumming & wailing from the other room.

No, no, no said Chelsea, this is so not happening.

I'll go talk to him, I said.

You better, she said. I have to get up for work in 5 hrs & I'll be goddamned if I'm going to lay here all night listening to that douche bag howl away like Satan's pet ferret.

I spent a few more minutes calming her down, then slipped on a robe & went out to the living room.

I had to raise my voice before Casper heard me.

He stopped mid verse & eyed me, blinking & expressionless, as if he intended to continue the song after I gave him whatever message I had to say.

Casper, I said, you're killing me. We're in there trying to sleep, remember? Casper looked confused. He had forgotten everything. He really believed that it was okay to sing & play the banjo on our couch in the middle of the night.

Sorry, he mumbled, sounding more embarrassed than apologetic. It's Ol' Gunner, he said, all of a sudden he had shit he wanted to say. He sat the banjo down on the carpet. I can't shut him up, when he wants to talk.

I rolled my eyes.

All right, I said, that's cool, whatever, just don't play the damned thing while you're in *my* home.

His eyes shot up & into mine. He'd felt the sting. I didn't know how to soften the blow & I didn't bother trying. I turned & went back to bed.

That following morning, when I re-entered the living room, Casper was still sitting Indian style on the couch, as if he hadn't slept at all. It didn't seem like he'd been reading, writing, watching television or anything. Just sitting.

I drove him to the train station. He only carried with him a shoulder bag & the guitar case with Gunner inside (it was a guitar case with a banjo inside, not a banjo case). If the shoulder bag was heavy, it was because of the books.

The station was dark & quiet when we arrived. Even the station clerks hadn't shown up yet. Casper plopped down on a bench & folded in his legs on the seat. He picked up the guitar case & cradled it.

I asked, are you good?

He nodded.

It was really good to see you, I said.

He nodded again. He didn't look at me.

As I was heading back to the car, I heard the banjo. Then Casper started wailing out with that voice of his, loud & high, like a baby demanding attention. I couldn't make out the lyrics. I don't know if they would have made any sense if I could have. I got into the car & drove to work. I fucking hate driving to work because the parking garages are a total rip off but oh well.

After work, I drove home. At home, I changed into my at-home clothes & washed my hands for dinner. At the kitchen table, Chelsea asked me how it was to see Casper again. Normally, she'd still be hounding me about last night, but, for the moment, she'd brought out the white flag. She could tell that something was bothering me.

I shook my head. All I could say was, meh, he hasn't changed at all.

My voice made it an insult; in my mind, it was a compliment. In reality, it was both. Or neither.

Chicago's Finest

Just as Officer Barron sunk my destroyer, Officer Rogers ran
in shouting, holy moley, chief, there's a humungous effing
robot on LaSalle and Monroe. You guys gotta see it he said,
it's freaking humungous! It was the third robot to invade the
downtown area in the last eight months. They're gigantic,
loud, clunky, and each one causes millions of dollars in
property damage. Every time, the phones ring off the hooks
like a symphony from hell. It's nerve wracking, but when
all's said and done it doesn't sour a day's work. When there's
a giant robot of doom on the rampage, we do the same thing
we do when there isn't a giant robot of doom on the rampage:
drink coffee and play Battleship. Here at home base, we're all
aces at Battleship. Challenge the CPD to a game of Battleship,
and that's your ass. You don't stand a chance. What a hell of a
game.

So I'm up against Officer Barron, he's whooping my tail and
the whole time Officer Rogers's shouting my ear off about the
new robot. Is Amazing Man there yet, I ask.

Not yet said Rogers, but the bet down in forensics is at 30/80.

30/80 means that it's gonna take Amazing Man thirty minutes
to hit the scene and eighty minutes to beat the robot. I want in
on that action, I said, there's no way he's gonna do it in eighty
minutes. How big is it?

About a third the size of the Hancock building said Rogers.
I'm not kidding chief, this one's big as shit.

What's the bid, I asked.

Seventy-five, said Rogers. I fished a few bills out my wallet and gave it to Rogers and said, 40/120. Officer Barron came up with another seventy-five to match mine.

Man's got a point, he said. Officer Rogers went down to forensics to get us into the pool.

I wanted to go see Amazing Man wrestle around with the robot. I missed the second one but the first was a hoot. Crazy robot was about to knock over the Sears Tower when Amazing Man climbed right up the mother and ripped it's head clean off. Oh man that was something.

About a half hour after he left, Rogers came racing back in saying this one's nasty, chief. It just took out the Picasso over at the Daley Center. Just stepped on the sucker, flattened it like a pancake.

Yeah yeah yeah I said, but did you get me in the pool? Officer Rogers gave me a blank look. You were supposed to get me into the pool. 40/120, remember?

Shoot said Rogers, and he took off.

I dunno chief said Officer Perry, who'd been sitting at the desk watching us play Battleship, I kinda almost feel like we should—

I cut him short.

Hey Perry, I said, why don't you be a dove and go fix me an espresso? We got an espresso maker in the kitchenette. Denver sent it over last Christmas. Those fellas are such sweetie pies.

Make mine a macchiato said Barron. A dozen other officers chimed in.

That's how it is really, even the officers who don't like coffee still like making the rookies bring them coffee.

Perry left to go get our drinks.

That was a close one, said Barron.

Close one, hell I said, and pointed to Barron's ships. You watch your ass.

Officer Perry came back awhile later and handed out our hot drinks. Like I was saying, chief, he said, shouldn't we be—

Bagels, I said. I think I can speak for everybody when I say the long arm of the law needs to reach out and grab some bagels. Officer Perry, if you wouldn't mind running along to the bagel shop?

It wasn't really a question. Officer Perry's face darkened as he left.

When Officer Perry brought back the bagels he launched back into it.

If I may, chief, he said. I don't think it's right that we're not doing anything about the robot.

Almost everyone in the room started laughing.

Give the rookie a break I said, chuckling.

By all means I told Perry, have at it, Gunga-Din. If you can arrest the unstoppable robot of doom, you can have my badge.

Mine too, said Rogers.

Mine too, shouted Nickels from the other end of the room.

There you go I said, go do your civil duty and you'll have three shiny badges waiting for you on your desk. You'll be a regular police constellation, all by yourself.

You're all a bunch of assholes said Officer Perry, storming off towards the men's room.

Gotta love the kid's spunk. He came in here wet behind the ears a few weeks ago and already we got him mouthing off.

Your move, I said to Barron, knowing he was about to sink my last dang sub. But then Officer Perry came back in a huff saying, no offense chief, but I think this is bull crap.

Hey hey I said, watch the language, young man. This ain't Kilroy's House of Cuss Words.

But sir, said Perry, I'm just saying. We don't do anything around here. A killer robot is on the loose in the downtown area and you guys are playing board games.

You see a board here, I asked, pointing to the table. Didn't think so. No board. There aren't any boards in battleship. Now why don't you go back to your desk like a good little boy and quit busting my balls.

But Perry still had that this-ain't-over look on his face so I said okay, listen kid. You wanna know what'll happen if we chase after that robot? We'll look like schmucks. Big time schmucks. We'll go down there and waste all our ammunition shooting at a clearly bulletproof robot, meanwhile the motherbutler starts stepping on us. When that part of the dummy circus ends, we'll start running around screaming, pissing our pants, until Amazing Man finally comes to save the day. At the end of the shift, those of us who didn't get squashed will end up going home with CHUMP tattooed on our foreheads. No thanks, kimosabee.

You know said Officer Barron, the kid's not way off though. Sometimes I do miss doing real police work.

Not me, I said, I did that crap for twenty-eight years. Lemme tell you, before Amazing Man came around, this job sucked. Say what you want about that drunken clown, but he's made our lives a heck of a lot easier. Before it was all bank robberies, shoot-outs, bomb threats. It wasn't like the traffic violations and parking tickets that we shuffle out now. I'm talking dangerous stuff here. Stacks of paperwork this high. Fighting crime is the bunk, pal, take my word for it.

I hear you said Barron, I just feel guilty sometimes is all. I mean, they probably still fight crime over in DC.

I picked up the phone at my desk and dialed up Carlos. Carlos was a chief over in DC. Hey Carlos, I said.

How the hell are ya Lou, said Carlos.

Oh, keeping it real, I said.

Hey, how deep is the shit over there?

Pretty deep said Carlos, damned rookie's got Broadway and Marvin Gardens already.

I put my hand over the receiver and nodded at Barron.

They're playing Monopoly.

In DC, Monopoly's the thing, not Battleship. In New York it's Stratego, in Los Angeles it's Risk and down in Dallas it's Scrabble. You gotta know which is which cause if you just waltz on down for a visit and a quick game or two, they're gonna hand you your behind and ship you right back.

Hey said Carlos, radio says you guys got a robot problem again. What are the odds?

I put down 40/120, I said. Carlos whistled.

You are going to lose that bet, my good man. Word is, Amazing Man's taking the Chief from Saint Louie. You know how Amtrak is, could be hours before he gets there.

Ah hell I said. Thanks, Carlos.

Two things never sleep, my friend, said Carlos. Rust and justice.

God bless it, I said, there goes my bet.

And there goes your battleship too, said Barron.

Son of a

Magical Sister Pants

By the time they entered high school, Lenise, Trudy and Simone were best friends. They had all met in kindergarten, become friends in grade school, and then play sisters in junior high. Now they were best friends, the dynamic trio, and each one believed that they'd stay best friends for always. They even bought a special pair of blue jeans to symbolize their unsinkable ship, their impenetrable fortress—sisterhood!

They found the blue jeans at a thrift store. The red price tag said six dollars and sixty-five cents, thank you very much.

The girls gave a name to the blue jeans: Travel Jeans.

After they bought the Travel Jeans, outside the thrift store, they held the Travel Jeans together and closed their eyes and chanted, 'Share the Travel Jeans together, stay friends forever!' They repeated it three times. Then they hugged one another. Later on, they were all embarrassed about how emotional they'd been. 'OMG,' they each thought, 'that was so hokey.' But at the time, it seemed very sweet and loving, and it made them feel that much closer to one another.

The Travel Jeans became their communal friendship jeans. Lenise would wear the Travel Jeans for a while, and then lend them to Trudy. Trudy would wear the Travel Jeans for a while, and then lend them to Simone. Simone would wear the Travel Jeans for a while, and then lend them to Lenise.

The Travel Jeans also represented female empowerment.

Lending out the Travel Jeans was a special event. If Trudy had a hot date, she would stop by Simone's house and say, 'I need the Travel Jeans tonight. For good luck.' Then, if Lenise was going on vacation with her parents, she would borrow the Travel Jeans from Trudy and wear them for the entire length of the vacation, each and every day, because when she wore the Travel Jeans she felt close to her best friends—no matter where she was.

Then, one fateful day: while Simone was on her way to Lenise's house to study for the physics exam, a low, hissing voice in her mind whispered *'Kill the jeans and gain its power...'*

The voice directed her to a trash can in front of a neighbor's house. Within the Rubbermaid trashcan was a jagged bronze dagger with an emerald embedded in the handle. *'Kill the jeans and gain its power,'* the voice urged once more. So Lenise decided that the only smart move was to head over to Trudy's house, steal the Travel Jeans and stab them to death with the dagger. 'Travel jeans,' thought Trudy, 'this blade shall be your gateway to hell!'

Only Trudy didn't have the Travel Jeans anymore. Simone had given her the Travel Jeans on the previous day, but after wearing them for an hour, a voice in Trudy's mind whispered, *'The jeans are stealing your life force. They can no longer be trusted.'*

And so, Trudy had changed out of the Travel Jeans and into her long jean-skirt. Then she lent the Travel Jeans to Lenise, and decided never to wear them again.

At Lenise's house, the Travel Jeans were wrapped around Lenise's ankles, as she sat on the toilet. Whilst defecating, Lenise was reading a novel by Neal Stephenson, a novel which everybody claimed was the greatest thing since sliced bread. Lenise thought it was decent enough, but certainly not on par with sliced bread.

It's rather hard to bump sliced bread out of the number one spot. After all these years, it still reigns undefeated.

When Lenise finished up, she stood, pulled up the Travel Jeans and fastened the crotch buttons.

Instantaneously, she disappeared.

The Travel Jeans knew that they were in danger. The clock was ticking. It was time to act.

The Travel Jeans began to run.

The Travel Jeans didn't really run. They forced Lenise's legs to run. And so, Lenise ran. She ran out of her house. Then she ran out of Moberly. Then she ran out of Maycomb County altogether. Then she ran out of Missouri.

The Travel Jeans let her stop running only when it realized that it was hundreds of miles away from harm.

And lost.

To make things worse, Lenise was completely helpless. She wanted to shed the Travel Jeans, but not only was she invisible—the Travel Jeans were also invisible.

She couldn't see where the crotch buttons were, to undo them. She couldn't even see where her hands were.

Back in Moberly, Simone and Trudy spent the evening at Trudy's house. Trudy's mom Miranda was out at the bars with her new boyfriend, so they went into the pantry and filched the fifth of rum and some diet cola.

Diet cola does not mix well with rum. But it was the only soda in the house.

With the rum and the diet soda and two plastic tumblers, Simone and Trudy went up into Trudy's room and proceeded to get wasted. And growl at each other like pirates. Because pirates drink rum.

'Aaargh,' said Simone, 'where be me Travel Jeans?'

'Methinks a l'il poppet ransacked the booty,' said Trudy. 'Aaaargh.'

'Aaarrgh,' said Simone, 'the scurvy dog! I swear by the sea, I'll finds me britches yet, and when I do, gonna plunge me dagger deep into its muddy black heart.' She was serious.

'I says, good riddance,' said Trudy, 'mark me words, them be haunted jeans. Cursed by the souls of the dead. Aargh.' She was also serious.

'Then ye won't be minding if I send the bloody jeans down to the house of Lucifer? Aarrgh,' said Simone.

'Do yer worst, wench,' said Trudy, 'ye do no harm by me.'

Later that night, Simone showed Trudy the dagger. Trudy threw her head back and laughed a big pirate laugh. *Ho Ho Ho!* It was a genuine laugh, and yet still a pirate laugh.

At that point, Trudy was far too intoxicated to take anything seriously.

'You look like a Wiccan priestess with that thing,' said Trudy, giggling in-between words. She did not say it in a pirate voice.

'Quit laughing,' said Simone, also laughing. 'I was gonna stab you, then steal the Travel Jeans and stab it to death. For realsies.'

'Whatever,' said Trudy. 'I bet you were going to try and sacrifice me to Goddess Midnight.'

'No I wasn't,' said Simone.

'Oh yeah,' said Trudy, 'the goddess needs her tribute o' blood.'

'Shut up, jerk,' said Simone.

Further into the evening, they ordered pizza. Pizza tastes delicious after several glasses of rum and diet cola.

Simone slept over at Trudy's house that night.

The next morning, both Simone and Trudy had monstrous headaches. They took turns vomiting in Trudy's bathroom.

Trudy's mother Miranda noticed that the rum was missing, but she didn't say anything about it—mostly because she felt guilty about being an alcoholic single-mother.

As they walked to the bus stop for school, Trudy and Simone both wondered what had happened to Lenise. She'd missed out on a fun night.

At that same moment, Lenise was wandering aimlessly about a vast expanse of empty land eighty miles out of Boise. She was famished, but she couldn't grab at anything to eat; being invisible shot her hand-and-eye coordination all to hell. And she kept tripping over rocks, every few steps, because she couldn't see her feet.

She wanted to take the Travel Jeans off. Unbutton them, peel them off and never wear them again. So desperately she wanted that.

But she should have been warned; what the Travel Jeans take, they never give back.

Not ever.

Lenise dropped to her knees, raised her skinny fists out to the sky and shouted 'No!' To be more accurate, it was more of a long, drawn out wail: 'Noooooooooooo!' If you could have seen it, it would have reminded you of heart-rending scenes from several dozen blockbuster movies. You're not much of a movie buff, but you've watched your fair share.

You've even thought to yourself before, 'Dang it, I've seen plenty of movies where someone drops to their knees, raises their fists to the sky, and shouts in agony—but I've never seen it happen in real life.'

But it's doubtful that you will ever see that, and you definitely could not have witnessed Lenise in such a pose. Lenise was invisible.

So much chaos, chaos borne of three friends that sought desperately to qualify platonic love. And qualify that love they did—with a pair of blue jeans purchased at a thrift store.

A thrift store built on Indian burial grounds.

Risk Management

You're saying, said Art Amberdink, CPCU, you work the mailroom at a law firm, don't have a degree, but you want a professional liability policy without a retro-date, and limits of… sorry, I'm reading the number here but I can't say it without laughing. Look, I'd help, Amazing Man, but—

I told you, said Amazing Man, I got no idea who you're talking about.

Right, said Art. You only resemble him. With glasses. Bet you hear that one a lot.

Tell me about it.

Why would Amazing Man need glasses anyhow? Surely super powers yield corrective vision.

I know, right?

Oh, my secretary forgot to inform you on the way in: I'm not a fucking idiot.

Art folded his arms, leaned back in his chair.

You're infamous among underwriters, you know.
No insurance company in the world will touch you. Not in the standard market. Not the E & S market. Nobody. Unknowingly insuring superheroes has ruined dozens of insurance companies. One claim—boom! Insolvency. And courts always sympathize with superheroes on extra-contractual damages.

Art shook his head.

No dice, Amazing—

I ain't Amazing Man! My name's—

That's right, Mr. Guy, Norm Guy. Hey, Norm—did you know? I'm a superhero. Behold my powers.

Frankie leaned towards the intercom.

Jackie, call security. We got another Johnny Wiseass in town.

Horton's Little Heaven

One time, at the bar, Horton reached into his pocket, pulled out his wallet. Take a look at this sweet mother, he said. In his wallet he kept a little plastic baggy, and in the baggy was a picture of somebody, and a small white feather. He wouldn't show me the picture. I saw a little bit of it, and when I pointed to it. Horton said, don't worry about that. Look at this. He showed me the feather. That was the sweet mother. A feather.

But see now, I never seen no feather like it before. Neither have you, whoever you are. It was a glowing piece of moon. A thin peel of sunlight. A hundred times brighter than any feather ought to be.

Came off an angel's wing, said Horton. My buddy Steve got it for me.

What's all that now, I said, some kinda bird, you say?

Ain't no bird he said, this here's a certified angel feather.

I grunted.

It's true, he said, holding it higher, letting it shine right up against my face. To hell with you, you don't believe me.

I asked him how in the sam hill his pal got hold of an angel's feather.

Steve kicked the bucket a year ago, said Horton, when that crazy bastard shot up all those people at the airport.

Jesus, I said.

Jesus ain't have nothin' to do with it, said Horton.

I kept quiet. Didn't know what to say to that.

Steve, he was one straight-shootin' son of a gun. God bless it. Rest in peace.

We raised our glasses to Steve.

When he got to Heaven, Horton said, he cased out the joint. First angel he saw, he rushed over, tore a feather off its wing and made a break for it. Got back down here and slipped it to me before they caught him.

Nobody made a stink about it? I asked.

Ah heck, said Horton, it's just one lousy feather. Those angels, they got feathers for days. What's just one? It don't matter to nobody, one feather. One feather means jack. He probably just had to say he's sorry, that's all that was. They don't hold no grudges up there.

I sipped my beer, thought a bit.

So why're you holding on to it, I asked. If it means jack, what's it to you?

Look at me, said Horton.

I looked at him. He was one ugly son of a bitch.

I'm one ugly son of a bitch, said Horton. Been this way all my life. But right now, see, I'm the only ugly SOB with this sweet mother.

It ain't real, I said.

What do you mean, said Horton, sure as heck, it's real. Just look at it. You look at it and tell me it ain't real.

I wanted to tell him so. I wanted to say, it's a fake, a big fat phony, anyone can see. Only looking at it, shining like that, whiter than ivory, whiter than any white I ever seen… I couldn't say nothing. I couldn't look away. I felt like, if I could only touch it, hold it for a few minutes, I would feel a little bit better. Everything would be better. Not so lonely.

Horton saw the way I was eyeing his feather. He quickly folded it up, stuffed it into the baggy, put the baggy back in his wallet and put his wallet back in his pocket.

Show's over, said Horton.

You know what, I said. I want it.

Huh, said Horton, peering over at me from the side of his eye.

I want that feather, I said, a little rougher.

No deal, said Horton. Get your own. This one ain't for sale.

I want it, I said. I been drinking with Horton for years, but all of a sudden I was ready to whoop him up real good over that feather. I can't explain myself no more than that.

Horton squinted at me.

I shouldn't have showed it to you, he said, if I'd a known you were gonna be a bastard about it.

Tell you what, I said, I'm gonna finish this beer. Then, I'm gonna go outside and wait in the parking lot. When you come out, either you hand over that feather or I'm gonna break your nose for you.

I finished my beer and Horton finished his beer and we went on outside.

He didn't hand over the feather and I didn't break his nose. I cuffed him one, in the shoulder. But Horton is one mountain of a man. A big ol' grizzly bear. It was a bum move to go pickin' a fight in the first place, but what can I say. The whiskey does funny things to a man.

All he needed was one good punch.

He got two.

I woke the next morning, up against the side of the Dodge. Most of the blood dried up overnight. My ears kept on ringing for three days straight.

Few weeks later, I saw Horton again at the bar. His cheeks were all black and blue, puffed up like a blowfish. I ain't do that, did I, I asked. Honest to God, I didn't remember.

He drank his beer, staring past the top shelf at stuff that wasn't there. He was good and sour about something.

I kept on staring.

He stopped ignoring me.

You can't have it, he said.

I don't want it no more, I lied. It's just a stupid feather. Bet you got it off a dead pigeon anyhow.

Yeah, uh-huh, whatever you say, said Horton. You can't have it no way.

He was trying to sound mean, but I knew something else was going on.

Oh yeah, I said, why's that?

I shouldn't even be talking to you, he said, you're just like every other bastard in the world.

I didn't say nothing to that, just waived Dom over for another Old Fashioned.

After a few minutes, Horton said, I got mugged last night. Rotten little punk stole my wallet. Got me good. Horton looked straight ahead, towards the top shelf.

I'm sorry, I said. I meant it.

More silence.

Hey, I said, maybe Steve will float on down and give you another feather.

Horton shook his head.

Don't think so, he said. Probably still knee deep in mess over the first one. I hope to hell they didn't kick him out.

Nah, I said, you can't get kicked out of Heaven. Horton frowned, eyed me for the first time that night.

Ain't never read the Bible, did you?

We talked a lot more than night, but it ain't really worth going into here. All I can say is, right around closing time, bygones were bygones. He wasn't so sore and I wasn't sore neither, except in the crotch. That part was still plenty sore. I swear, Horton knows how to kick alright. But I wasn't mad, is what I mean.

While I was in whizzing in the john that night, I started thinking. When I got back to the bar, I said to Horton, hey, I got an idea. How about this. One of us dies, he's gotta do it all over again. The whole con. I bet I could get my hands on a couple feathers, if I really tried. One extra, for back-up.

Don't need no damned feathers, said Horton. You steal one, you keep it to yourself.

Alright now, I said, what's going on here? We're still talking about a feather, ain't we?

Never mind all that crap, he said, waiving it off. Look here. Kept a picture of my little girl in that wallet. I ain't seen Janey in, hell, going on seventeen years. Only picture I had. He shrugged. You could snatch off a whole wing, all I care.

I mean it. Rip the whole sucker off, Fed Ex it on down to me. Don't mean a thing. You get me back my picture, then we got a deal. The picture, that's what it's all about.

I know I'm gonna die one day. After that, who needs a stupid old feather. They got angels flying around up there. Hundreds of feathers on 'em, each one. But that picture, I won't never get that back.

I scratched my head. You know, I said, you could always go and find your daughter. She's still alive, ain't she? Horton nodded.

Far as I know, she's hitched up with some ass wiper up on the north side.

Well then, I said, hell's so great about a picture? Real McCoy is walking around out there. Right now.

Horton gave me a real thick, metal face. You don't know nothing about nothing, he said. He didn't say another word to me.

That's the truth alright, though. What do I know? I know squat. All I know now is, when I get to Heaven, I ain't stealing nothing for nobody. What people really want, it's on Earth already, no matter what it is, even if it's stupid, and it usually is.

Letters to The Superhero from Elementary School Students

Dear Amazing Man,

Thank you for saving my life. We kids were all scared but you saved us from that big train. It almost smashed our bus to pieces! We would have kicked the bucket. Now we are still alive and it is because of you. Thank you so much for not letting us get squished and die. Everyone in my class which is Mrs. Peterson's 5th grade home room class is very happy we got to see you in person since your so awesome and famous. I never saw a superhero before but your one. Now we can say that we saw Amazing Man in person and he saved us like superheroes do. It is even O.K. that after you saving us you barfed everywhere. No problem. Even us kids barf sometimes. Joey Bamba barfed too right on the bus and it was nasty. But he only barfed cause he saw you barf and that was so bad. But thank you anyways cause looking at barf is better than kicking the bucket. And finally I am sorry that we were not nice to you.

Sincerely,
Lisa G.

P.S. – I never went #2 in my pants and if anyone says so he is a liar.

***

Dear Amazing Man,

Thank you for saving my life. And you also saved every kid on the bus. In the bus where all of the kids in Mrs. Peterson's 5th grade class. That is 36 kids.

We were going to the Museum of Science and Industry but the bus driver said that if it were not for you we would have all gone to Heck instead.

The bus broke down on the train tracks and we were all supposed to get squashed like grapes when the train came but then you showd up and saved us. We were all very scared. You don't look like you do in the pictures but that's good. I thought you wore a black cape all the time but in real life you had on a bathrobe like my mom wears. It was funny looking but Mrs. Peterson said you probably did not have time to get your cape because you were busy saving people. That's cool. Oh and also you puked everywhere and that was the best part! I'm not sorry because when everyone else made fun of you I thought it was cool looking. So in confusion remember that I was not mean to you.

Your friend,
Tommy

***

Dear Amazing Man

Thank you for saving my life. Mrs. Peterson told us to write this letter for homework so I am writing it. It was the worst field trip ever but we are not dead so great. Everyone was crying and screaming and the bus driver shouted bad words. The train almost hit us and then you came out of nowhere and stood in front of the train and stopped it with your two hands. That was nice I guess but then Joey Bamba horked and Lisa Gallows pooped her pants so the whole bus was stinky.

And you horked too and that was so gross because you horked for so long time and I had not seen anyone hork up so much before. When I told my Dad the story he said he bet you got too sauced up last night. He said sometimes when you hit the bottle the bottle hits you back. I don't know what that means but it did look like somebody hit you with a big bottle. And why was you wearing a robe? You are supposed to wear a cape. Plus the robe was green and your colors are gray and black and we all know that. But anyway it was a day I will not forget and thank you. And I am sorry that we were all mean to you.

Sincerity,
George P.

***

Dear Amazing Man,

Thank you for saving my life. Wow I can not believe it. I have all your comic books and I know all about you and it is so cool but now I can say that you saved me too! My class was going to the Museum of Science and Industry on a field trip and the bus broke down in the middle of the railroad tracks. All us kids thought we were doomed but you came all a sudden and stopped the train with your hands. Cool beans! Mrs. Peterson wanted us all to thank you for our homework today but I wanted to write you anyhow. When the whole story was on the news my mom taped the whole thing on tape. One thing was that my stepdad Jared said that you looked like h e double hockey sticks and then he called you two bad words. But don't listen to him because he is not nice.

But he is right about one thing you did throw up after all so maybe you should see a doctor. Also last of all I am sorry that all of us were making awful sounds after you threw up everywhere. We should not have done that cause then you gave us the finger and went away mad. I am sorry and hope that your not still mad. I am your big fan and always will be your big fan. I want to be just like you one day. I just hope that I do not throw up when I save people.
Thank you very much.

Sincerely,
Sheldon V.

***

Dear Amazing Man,

Thank you for saving my life. You probably won't even read this and some sectary is probably going to throw all this letters away. But thank you. That kicked butt was great when you stopped the train. I am sorry that you vommitted everywhere but that was almost great because you did it for so long. I am sorry that we were mean. You should not have pointed your middle finger at us because that was mean too. But I am glad anyway and also I think your new costume is weird. My gandma has a costume just like yours and she wears it every single day so maybe she is a superhero too ha ha. I am just kidding. I also really hope that this is long enough because Mrs. Peterson told all of us in the class that we had to write this letter for two hundred words for homework and if this is not long enough I will not getting full credit.

So in conclusion thank you very much, and please tell Mrs. Peterson to take us go back to the museum again because they are showing dead people where you can touch them and we didn't get to go today

and I want to touch dead people and stuff. Thank you. And I am sorry again for how mean we were.

Sincerely,
Bill F.

Curse

I wasn't trying to hit nobody. She came outta nowhere. I
didn't do anything wrong. The truth? She had a death wish.
That's what I think. But right at the end she was steady trying
to blame me, just in case Jesus or somebody was looking.
And even if it was my fault—and it wasn't my fault—shit
just happens sometimes. You can't blame nobody. There's
no good or evil—just shit.

Her boy Bence said she was always cursing folks out, for
anything. Most times, her heart wasn't even in it. After she
put a hex on somebody, hour later, she was cool again. Half
the time, she didn't even remember who it was got all up in
her business. That was just her way, Bence said. My mother,
she was gangster. He said it just like that.

I said, but what if she meant it this time? Out of all the
times she cursed somebody, this is the only time she cursed
a brother that hit her with a bus. That might change shit.

Bence shook his head.

I can offer you no peace of mind, my friend. This is very
serious. A true curse is no joke.

I don't know how long I have. It could be three days or it
could be a year. I won't even know. One day, somehow,
I'm going to come up short.

I didn't believe it right up front. Bence was like, they are
real, my friend. This is why you do not fuck around with old
Romani women. They play no games.

He showed me pictures of what happened to other brothers that got jacked up. Shit was cold-blooded. She wasn't stingy with those curses neither. It was like she was doing it just to do it.

Well, said Bence, there is a lot, but what you do not see are all the people she only pretended to curse. These, they are the real curses. Many times, she was not sincere.

Ah ha. See now. There was one man, said Bence, he was very mean to her. He shouted at her and then spit in her face. My mother put a terrible curse on this man.

Bence shook his head.

One week later, he said, this man blew up.

I didn't know what that meant.

What does that mean, blew up?

Bence pointed to one picture.

You see? He blew up.

I saw.

What in the fuck do you even say to that.

But then, Bence said, she also cursed the landlord after we were evicted. She said his heart would turn to ice one day. Twenty years later, this man is still alive. Bence put his hand on my shoulder. At least you have a chance, my friend.

Bence is alright. He tries to act like he's black sometimes, but he's cool. He's one of the chillest cats I've ever met. He didn't even hold anything over me.

My heart is broken, he said, I do not have a mother now. But she was very old. This is the way of life. Shall I put another hex on you? No. Your doom has been sealed. I am only sorry, as I can offer you no help, my friend.

I will say this though. I don't worry bout nothing anymore. When I got laid off the public transit, I thought, fuck it, I'll be dead soon anyway. Credit card bills? Later for all that shit. One day, it won't matter anymore. The fuck can they do? Cancel my shit? My shit has already been cancelled. They can't get me. I've already been got.

I don't stress about not a damn thing now. I only do what I feel like doing. If I feel like sleeping all day, I sleep all the god damn day. I'm about broke and can't even come up with the rent, but fuck it. The best time in the world is when you can look at every problem you have and just say fuck it all. I don't even need to drink to feel like this.

The other day, I had dinner at an Indian restaurant. Never had Indian food before. I've been driving buses past this one place for a long ass time, always thinking about what Indian food tastes like. Then I went past it and was like, let me get at this before I blow the hell up. And yeah, okay, I don't really like it. Shit is way too mushy. They kill it with that curry. But fuck it. Now I know.

Next week, me and Bence are hitting up a hookah bar. I don't even smoke anymore but he said that hookahs are The Truth.

He said it like that, like, you are going to love it, my friend. Hookah bars, they are The Truth. The way he talks is a trip. They are The Truth, my friend. Just like that. That shit has me rolling every time.

Room for Buddies

Everyone knows that the Buddy Room is a gay bar, but what everyone doesn't know is that it's also a popular vampire hangout. From ten or so at night to three in the morning, it's jam packed with vampires. I know this because… well it's complicated. I'm not gay and I'm not a vampire. I'm pretty sure. About the gay part. Positive about the vampire part. But, you see…one morning, I got out of bed, went to the bathroom and looked in the mirror. All I saw was my big fat gut and my receding hairline and the big white first-degree burn mark on the left side of my face, the one that I can't cover up no matter what, not with a beard, not with glasses, and not with a beard and glasses and long hair. I looked at all of that and I wanted just one person to not care about it, to treat me like I was special, like I wasn't a stain on the couch of life.

Vamp tramp. That's what they call a woman who has a fetish for vampires. I suppose the same name could be used for a man too. But I don't think there's a name for straight men who pretend to be gay to lure gay vampires into whisking them away and sucking their blood.

Yes, I know that sounds masochistic and morbid, but it's not really. Well, yes it is, but I can explain. Sort of. See, vampires don't have sex. They don't have a sex drive. They might have sex because they have a thing for the act itself, but there's no libido, they derive no physical sensation from it. I know there's all that bull malarkey that you see in books and movies, but come on, why would an immortal creature have a sex drive when it doesn't reproduce? That's just silly. On top of that, it's very rare that a vampire kills.

They usually just suck a pint or so of your blood and leave you somewhere indiscreet. It's like that old urban legend of waking up in a tub full of ice without a kidney—only you get to keep your kidneys. It's similar to donating blood. Okay, yes, now and then you have to watch out for a psycho, but it's no different with regular people.

I can relate to people who get off on drugs. With heroin junkies, after a while, it's not even the heroin that they go crazy over. It's the point of impact when the needle pierces the skin. It's the whole process of cooking up, drawing, finding that vein--it's the journey, not the destination. I get that. It's the same with vampires: it's the courtship, the subterfuge, the walk back to the car, the hotel, the alley. It's the burst of euphoria when a vampire's fangs clamp down on your jugular vein. You feel a rush, like an electric current flowing through you, before a deep sense of fatigue sets in and you float away.

I want to say that their fangs are coated with a type of fluid that induces sleep, an anesthesia. Have to read up more on that.

I was nervous in the beginning. I kept thinking, I must look dreadfully out of place here. They will take one look at my stupid blue shirt and my stupid shoes and will know that I'm not gay. That's what I really thought, that I would set foot in the place and a gay detector would sound off and I'd get kicked out. Red alarms flaring. Intruder! Intruder! But it wasn't like that. Everyone was nice. I never had to buy a drink; guys kept offering to buy for me. There was a lot of flirting, but nobody was ever pushy or overbearing. I had great conversations about baseball, movies and politics.

Then, when someone asked for my number, I'd say no thanks, sorry. Very friendly, very good-spirited.

All it took was one vampire and one too many drinks. He was bald with a goatee and sparkling green eyes. Towards the end of the night, he said hey, I want to show you something. He led me out to the alley behind the bar, and I thought, oh boy, what have I gotten myself into? He pinned me against the wall. Licked his lips. The next thing I knew, it was morning, and I sitting on the ground between two trash cans. The whole right side of my neck was caked up with blood. The vampire had left a little note in the breast pocket of my shirt. It read

Thank you, you're a dove. Be sure to drink lots of fluids today!

I started going to The Buddy Room once a week. That was my limit; I wanted to make sure I wasn't losing too much blood. But from that night on, I started cruising for vampires. I never saw the first one again, but there were plenty of others out there. And picking out the vampires in the room is easy once you get the hang of it. There were some hiccups in the beginning. I got myself into a few jams where I had to say sorry, friend, you're a sweetie, but you're not really my type. Something to that effect. An easy letdown.

Over time, I could walk into a room and pick out the vampires. It's not like in the movies. You can't point out the pale guy and say it's him, he's the bloodsucker. They don't look any different than regular people. But they have a swagger, a graceful movement. Glint in the eyes. And vampires lick their lips way more than regular people.

They do it really quickly, like a snake.

I was routine about it, my trips to the Buddy Room, for six months or so. Maybe longer. Probably longer. I don't know how long exactly. Then, well, then a lot of stuff happened. I just... maybe cruising and having one night stands with the undead gets to you after a while. Maybe losing so much blood made me constantly woozy, night and day, and crazy ideas got into my head. But around that time, that's also when my cousin Clark died of cancer, and then, while driving to work one morning, I saw this kid swerve his car off the expressway and down into a quarry. I was several cars away, but I saw the whole thing. I've never seen anything like that before.

On the news, all I heard about was death. Teenage suicide rate increasing. The O'Hare Massacre, where an illegal immigrant shot a ton of people at the airport. Hundreds and hundreds of thousands dead in Darfur. Death in Iraq. Death in Afghanistan. Death by Earthquakes. Death by hurricanes.

I felt like death was all around me, everywhere, in the air. And what was I doing, all that time, with death touching everyone around me? I was slutting myself out, letting any old vampires have a go at me, suck a little bit of life out of me, a little once a week. I started to think, how can I get away from all this death in the air, death in the water? What if I became a...?

But vampires hate that, they hate turning humans into vampires. It seems simple enough. They suck your blood, you suck theirs, wait a little bit—presto, new vampire. No sweat off their backs. But no. Vampires hate hate hate it. It's because they don't like the idea of having to deal with one more jerk for all of eternity. It's easy to tolerate humans.

Even the most annoying human on the face of the planet will only live for about three-fourths of a century, give or take. To a vampire, that's not very long. An annoying vampire, however, could very well stay annoying forever. You can avoid him for a while, but then three, four, five hundred years later, he's right back in your face, and you have to deal with his B.S. all over again.

Vampires catch on quickly enough, so you have to be a really good actor. Over the course of a millennium or two, vampires become rather perceptive. All it takes is one goofball comment, and everything's fubar. Like if I said, man, I just feel so passionate about life these days. There's so much to do, so many places in the world I haven't seen. I just wish life wasn't so short. Know what I mean? If I said that to a vampire, his whole attitude would turn on a dime. He'd become cold and curt with me, probably excuse himself to the restroom and disappear. Or else he'd turn away abruptly and go talk to someone else at the bar. Even if I tried to cover it all up and say, but hey, that's what life is all about, right? Carpe diem? It would be too late. In the vampires eyes, I'd see, he'd be on to me. His eyes would said sorry, pal, deal's gone bad.

Then, I met a guy.

He was a really tall, handsome guy; bandana, tattoos on both arms, tongue ring, clean-shaven. We hit it off right away, so much so that I wanted to buy him drinks all night—which I never do. We talked about traveling. He'd lived in Japan, Italy, Germany, China, Spain. He loved to hike. He was learning Sanskrit, practiced yoga and meditated. When I handed him drinks, he touched, no, caressed my fingers as he'd take the glass away.

He always held eye contact when he listened to me speak, never took his eyes away from me. His eyes were crystal blue, and had that feral gleam about them. Serpentine tongue. Elegant, smooth disposition. No doubt about this one.

We had a table to ourselves way off in the corner of the bar, just talking, and we went on and on for most of the night. Did I like Thai food? Camping? Okay, if I wasn't stuck here and could go live in any other city, where would I go?

I kept waiting, okay, who was going to make the first move? One of us had to, so that we could go someplace quiet and get down to vampire business. But he made no proposal, and, for some reason, neither did I. Over all that, the conversation was just... I liked talking to him. We connected.

At one point, he reached out and touched the burn mark on my face, just one delicate touch.

What happened here, he asked. Just like that. I told him the whole story, about my step-brother and the fire. I'd never told the whole story to anyone.

When I was done, his eyes were trembling and he whispered shaaa-duh. I didn't know exactly what it meant at the time, ut I looked it up later and it's about what I presumed.

Finally, around two in the morning or so, I said to him, look, I've a confession to make.

He smiled and said, so do I.

I said, please, let me go first.

I have to get this out. I'm not gay.

The smile didn't leave his face.

Also, he said, in that case, I have two confessions. One, he said, is that I realized this, that you are not gay, almost two hours ago. And this is my other confession. I am not a vampire.

We left The Buddy Room to go get coffee. It was okay to stay out a little later. Neither of us had to worry about daybreak.

Constantin was an accountant. He was from Frankfurt, but had lived in the United States for the last eleven years. It's funny, I had no idea he was German. He spoke with almost no accent. Even after I knew that he was German, it was barely perceptible in his voice, even as I tried to listen closely for it.

He'd been going to The Buddy Room for a couple years now. There were others; he frequented a lot of gay vampire bars, and told me about some of the better, lesser known ones. This is one of the reasons I moved to the United States, he said. In Germany, there are almost no vampire bars. Maybe three, in the entire country—all in Berlin. In the United States, you have many of them in every major city. The world knows this. The United States is the vampire capitol of the world.

Constantin said that he'd seen me at the bar plenty of times. He'd wanted to say something to me but never found the chance. Like me, he hooked up with vampires, whatever 'hooked-up' means. Sometimes, though, he went home with regular men; sometimes he went home with vampires.

Then, sometimes, he went home with a regular guy who thought he was a vampire. You can't fool other vampires, he said, but it's really easy to imitate the vampire look and fool other men.

But, I said, what about the bloodsucking bit? How do you pull that off? His face reddened a little, sheepishly.

I never suck the blood, he said. What is the saying? I slip them a mickey. When I see that it is about to set in, I start to bite.

Then Constantin got on the defensive. That is where it ends, he said. I do nothing... unpleasant. I have a set of fake fangs. I make one small bite, and then stop the blood very quickly. Then, I leave.

Why bother, I said? He made a sour face.

Why do you bother? If you are not gay and you not a vampire, it seems to me that you could... how do you say, cut out the middle man? You could visit your local blood bank.

Touché, I said. Touché indeed.

We made plans to meet again, a couple nights later.

At the end of the night, or rather in the morning, we left the café, embraced and parted ways. It felt good to hug him. It had only been one night, but I felt close to him. Sharing my secret was so refreshing, such a load off. Like letting out a deep sigh, or undoing your belt buckle after work. I wasn't even that disappointed that the night hadn't ended with any blood-letting.

I thought about it all week at work. Did this mean I was gay? I had enjoyed talking to him. The hug, it stayed in my mind, in the center. Maybe it just felt good to hug anyone, to feel that closeness to another person, another warm body. It had been a long time since I felt that. I remember once, at the same coffee shop, I saw a young African-American lady and an old white guy meet up by the booth next to mine. Before sitting down, they greeted each other in some foreign language and then locked in a big, tight hug. I tried not to stare, but I thought, wow, how happy they must be to have that. Maybe they were lovers? Most likely, he was her coworker, her stepdad, something like that. Even still. I've never hugged anyone like that. There are hugs and then there are hugs. There are really casual hugs, formal hugs, friendly hugs. But the real ones, deep ones, they are wonderful and you can't deny them. But hugging a man like that, enjoying it like that… was I gay?

The voice in my head said, come on, pal, you go to gay bars, flirt with gay men, let gay men hit on you and hmm, let's see, you get your rocks off when vampire men bite your neck and suck your blood. Then, on top of that, you have the hots for a gay German. If all of that doesn't make you gay, then there is no such thing as gay.

Only, I liked women. I did. Or I was attracted to them. Sure, being around women made me skittish. More like petrified. My hands get all clammy and I stutter and say nonsense. On the street or downtown by my office building, I see beautiful women all the time. I stare and think man, I wish I weren't so ugly. Then I'd have a chance with women like that.

I could have probably found the bars where all the female vampires go.

Straight bars, that is, where female vampires pick up straight guys, or vice versa, depending on how you want to look at it.

But that seems too intimidating to me. I had my whole game down pat at the Buddy Room. I could go to the Buddy Room and not feel like everyone there was staring at my burn marks. No one was going to take one look at me and say no thanks, I can do better than a chubby chub like you. But with girls, er, women, I'd spill beer on myself, or spit would fly out of my mouth when I talked, or… or… it probably wouldn't even go that far; most girls, I bet, would look at my cheap shoes and walk away. Somehow, they would know immediately that I was only the what's-it-guy from the mail room.

I even tried to be gay. I did. One night at home, in bed, I concentrated really hard on the image of naked men, and tried to see if that got anything moving downstairs. It didn't. Then I thought about Constantin. Holding him again, hugging him. It was comforting, that thought. Warm, strong. Still, nothing happening below the belt, but… I wanted to see him again. I wanted to hold him, feel my cheek against his. Run my fingers against his lips. Feel those lips against mine.

He stood me up for our next date. I went to the Buddy Room and waited for him. And waited. And waited.

At midnight, I stopped waiting.

I still went out after that. Couple times a week. But I couldn't focus. Never hooked up. I kept looking for Constantin. Other guys would offer to buy me drinks. No thanks, I'd say.

Even when I was able to strike up casual chit-chat, it was always obvious that my mind was elsewhere, and the other guy would eventually catch on that I was waiting for someone.

I did see him again. Months later. I walked into one of the other bars, The Silver Bullet, and right away I saw him by the counter, hob-knobbing with a group of posh, hoity-toity vampires. He glanced at me, gave a brief nod, then turned his back. He didn't seem surprised or excited. I can't blame him. Our reason for connecting so well that one time was also a good reason never to talk to one another again.

I don't like the scene so much anymore. I still go to The Buddy Room now and again. Not often. Not even once a month. Once in a blue moon. Occasionally, I'll hook up with a vampire. I'll let him do his thing, and I'll wake up the next morning in an alley, a hotel room. It's passable… but it's also routine and formulaic. Leaves me feeling a little sad. It was always a charade, but now that it feels like a charade, it's no fun.

Maybe it's better that I'm not a vampire. Wouldn't want to feel this way forever.

The Super Deal

My son Danny thinks he got heat ray vision. Well he says, his
super power is heat ray vision—it just ain't kicked in yet. Any
day now, he's gonna start shooting heat rays from out his eyes.
Heat rays all over the place. Big ol' heat rays. Hottest heat rays
you ever saw. But, oh wait. I'm not s'posed to call him Danny
anymore. He's Pyro Boy.

You know where he gets it from? It's that bear-humping
superhero. Back when I was a kid, someone asked me, what
d'you wanna be when you grow up? I said a fire fighter, just
like every kid's s'posed to say. Every little boy was gonna be
a fireman and every little girl was gonna be a nurse. Period.
End of story. But now every ankle-biter in the world just has
to be a superhero. Firefighting ain't hip enough no more.
Don't help that half these kids got gummy bears for brains.
Just last month, there was this real screwed up story all over
the news. A milk truck in the Loop went haywire and ran over
two people, an old lady and a kid. The twisted part is, it only
shoulda hit the old lady. The kid saw the truck coming and
thought he could save the granny by jumping in front of her
and stopping the truck with his Super Hands. The truck killed
the kid, killed the granny, then crashed into a coffee shop and
sent six more people into the hospital.

That's one story. The papers are full of them, more and more
coming out every day. The whole country's going down the
crapper cause everybody wants to be a superhero.

But Danny…I thought Danny would take over the business
after I retired. That's the whole flipping reason I named it
De Gooning & Son, Instead of just De Gooning.

But now, shucks, now Idunno. Danny—I mean Pyro Boy—
don't give two farts about woodwork. I can slap together one
hell of an oak armoire, ask anybody in town. Under my wing,
Danny was gonna make even tougher armoires. I'm talking
armoires to beat the band. But that's Danny. I dunno about
Pyro Boy. Pyro Boy, I don't want that nutso anywhere near
my shop.

I had this nightmare. I was in the backyard, drowning in the
pool. Right over me, at the edge of the pool looking down,
was Danny. He had his arms stretched out, wiggling his little
fingers. Go-go heat vision, he said. The heat rays were s'posed
to shoot out his eyes and into the pool and evaporate all the
water. That's how the little turd was gonna save me. I shouted
Danny, for the luva Pete, give me your hand! But Danny
didn't budge, just kept wiggling those fingers. Have no fear,
Pyro Boy is here! And so I sunk like a cement block, right
down to the bottom of the pool. Then I woke up.

My wife Claire says it's a phase. Says kids can't tell who the
real heroes are 'til they grow up. Sounds sweet. It does. But
me, I always figured part of growing up is finding out, there
ain't no real heroes, just lucky guys and unlucky guys. It's like
my old man used to say. He said, you can't save the world—it
ain't for sale. Idunno what it meant, but there's truth in there
somewhere. Tell you what though. I know what is on sale:
my armoires. You won't find better armoires nowhere else in
Chicagoland. That's a promise. Long as Pyro Boy doesn't burn
down the place, De Gooning & Son will always be the last
stop for sturdy, handmade oak furniture sold at competitive
prices. I won't save your life, but I might save you a couple
of bucks. That's why our mascot's a buck. The buck stops at
De Gooning & Son. You ever make it to Calumet City, stop by.

Strawberry

My kindergarten teacher Ms. Carbunkle was a cocaine addict.
Everything else about her was strawberry. She was shaped like
a strawberry. Her cheeks & lips were strawberries. She wore
strawberry dresses, earrings &—outside during recess—knit
strawberry hats. Her strawberry voice loved everyone.

One day after school I forgot my backpack. I ran back to class
and saw Ms. Carbunkle, hunched over her desk, snorting
snowflakes off a little mirror. Then she smiled a strawberry
smile.

At home I cried for hours. I didn't understand anything then.
Now I know. Teachers & everyone else are both wonderful &
awful.

Chance of a Lifetime

You meet lots of kooky people, you go to a bar often enough.
This bar right here, maybe it's queer duck central. Feels like
it anyway. All kind of characters show up. Saw a guy dressed
up like a caped crusader. 'Nuther night, this drunk old lady
was going around saying oooh, I'ma werewolf, better not
come round me when the full moon's out, or I'll bites youse.
Like I say, queer duck central. But that's why I like the place.
Better'n TV. Better'n staying home, that's for goddamn sure,
hollering at my old lady. Worst of it, my wife, she's a mind
reader. Sometimes, we get to shouting over something that I
thought. Don't even gotta say it. It's no good. Better at the bar.
I can order a cold one, know it's all gonna go down smooth.

This one time, I come in for a cold one, warm me up for the
road home. Winter came'n snuck up from behind, gave a tap
on the shoulder and clocked us all one right in the nose. Even
in my new thermal coat and my sister-in-law's ugly scarf, I
was freezing my buns off, working out in the yards all day.
Right at eight I clocked out and head on over to Binky's, took
my usual seat at the counter and said good googley moogley!
The hawk is out there tonight.

Yes, sir, said Dominic, the bartender.

I like Dom. He's as surly as he is Irish, and he's plenty Irish.

It's colder than hell tonight, he said. It gets this icy, brother,
you can rest assured, Lucifer's sneaking up on you.

Roger, good buddy, I said. Sure feels like it.

Feels like it, my arse, said Dom. I'll swear to the book, brother. I tell no tale. We're in the very presence of the Devil himself tonight.

Now don't get all carried away Dom, I said, it's that cold time of the year, and that's all there is to it.

Your mother's getting carried away, said Dom. I tell you, the Devil is with us this night! You don't believe me, brother, you can go and ask him yourself.

Where is he?

Dom pointed to the far end of the counter.

Right over there.

I looked down the counter. Was just this little guy, squirrely fella, with balding flames of red hair, bad skin and a couple specks of a beard. Not too clean a mug.

All the same, he ain't really strike me as the prince of darkness or nothing.

I felt like jawing it up a bit, so I scoot on over to the guy and said to him, I said, whatcha drinking?

Cranberry juice, he said.

The hell's that about? You on your period?

Easy, partner. It's all the same to me. Can't get myself drunk no how, no matter what it is. This here's good as anything.

Hey Dom, I said, another brewski for me, and a cranberry juice for my compadre here. So, I say, turning back to the guy, word is, you're the Devil.

The guy shrugged.

That's the word on the street, he says.

Word on the street also has it, you're the reason why it's s'dang cold 'round here.

The guy nodded.

Yeah, sorry about that. That's all me. I screwed you guys on that one. Don't know what to tell you, amigo. I go somewhere, everything gets colder than it oughta be. Just how it is. Can't help it.

I wanted to get a little bit more bang for my buck out of all this, so I said to the guy, I said, yeah, so what brought you here anyway?

Just passing through, he said. On my way back home. It's been a mother of a day. This Red Paper Chase I was working overtime on, it just went belly up.

Red Paper Chase, I said, what's that now?

Ah, pardon me, he said, that's business lingo, right there. What I call a deal where's I get some chump to sign over his soul, trade it off for something worldly, you know, fortune and glory. Red Paper Chase. Red, on account of I used to make 'em sign with a red ink pen.

114

Little bit of symbology, you know? Don't do that so much now, scared off a lot of folks. Lost too much business that way. Chase, cause I have to spend the rest of their lives chasing them 'round, make sure they keep to the contract, don't play wise with me. And paper, well, the contract's on paper.

No kidding, I said. This was getting good. So, let me get this straight, I said, you really think you're the Devil?

Stared me straight down, eye to eye. I saw the flames licking up from in each pupil. Off, just as far away as I could hear, just the faintest screams and madhouse laughing. Boiling blood and claws and hissing. All in them two eyes.

He winked.

Yeah, it was him alright.

Well I'll be damned, I said.

Lemme see what I can do, he said. Sipped his juice.

So you tried to get some sucker to sell away his soul?

Didn't say that, he said. Didn't try to, I did it. I got the idiot to sign away. Signed, sealed and delivered. Lousy good for nothing soul oughta be tucked away in my back pocket right now.

What happened, I asked.

I'll tell you what happened, he said. I got the shaft is what happened. Big time shaft.

See here, I find myself a real card, young fella, plenty smart, still lived in his Ma's basement. That's my bread and butter, unrealized potential, them little lambs what don't know what they got going for 'em. Meat and potatoes, right there. His name was Buddy, but I call him Dinkus, on account of the kid was a real Dinkus alright.

I didn't even find him; he called me. Guy spent all his days working on a whole lotta nothing. All he did was read them comic books and look at nudie pictures on his computer box, all day long. Wondered why his life didn't go nowhere. Didn't have no friends, no buddies, no little lady on his shoulder. He had his Ma and his stag reels, is all he had. Well, one day, he got on his knees and said, 'I'd sell my soul to the Devil for things to turn out okay for me, every once in a while.' Well, abbra cadabbra, I showed up right then and there, dressed to the nines, like I do. Came in a puff of smoke, the good old way. Told the kid, well hello now, I think I might be the gentleman you're after.

Been offering these kinda deals for a while. All your earthly dreams will come true. You want fame? Fortune? Wanna get your kicks? Need some good, clean girls to do the dirty with you? I'll make it happen. Alls I ask is that when you bite the bullet, I get your soul for keeps. Quid pro quo. You get a lot now, I get a little bit later.

This kid, Dinkus he had this smart alec grin all over his face. It's always the same thing with these kids, all think they're the bee's knees. Been like that for thousands of years. They think, oh, tra la la, I don't believe in Heaven and Hell, so what's it to me if I sell some sucker my soul?

116

Heck of a lot of nerve, you ask me, but I don't say nothing about that, it's all part of the game.

Gotta play out the hand. So boy genius took the bait, signed on the dotted line and dated it. You're doing the right thing, amigo, I said, and gave him a hearty old handshake. Get ready for the good old days.

And so, I said. Did you keep your end?

That's where sugar turned to shit, he said. Now look here, thing about the contract, it's missing a clause. Fucking regulation department's going to hear when I get back home, lemme tell you, they ain't gonna be happy to see me. The contract, it only talks about the chump that's gotta keep up his part of the bargain. My part, well, I got all the smoke and mirrors down pat, so you don't see too much about that end of it. You know, my end of the bargain oughta be the easy end. But I shit you not, the whole universe fought me on this one. I just could not make life turn around for that cheesehead.

What do you mean, I asked. All you had to do was make a big sack of money magically appear right in front of him.

I'm telling you, amigo, said the Devil, as sure as I'm sitting here, I do believe if I had done that, the sack would've caught fire and burned down to ashes. Don't ask me how, it just would've happened that way.

See now, the first time, I tried to take it nice and easy. He always bought a lottery ticket at the corner store a block from his Ma's house. I rigged it so that the next ticket he bought would've been a winner.

What happened? He bought it, scratched and chucked it, all in 'bout a minute. Three million dollars, right in the dump.

Why'd he throw it away?

Son of a monkey bar didn't even look at it, he said. Got so used to scratching off instant lottery tickets, he didn't even pay attention to them no more.

So what did you do then?

What didn't I do? I got some suit on the payroll to show up at his door, say excuse me, your distant Uncle So and So just bit the big one, and he left his whole inheritance to you. What's that, he said? There must be some mistake. Ain't got no Uncle So and So. End a' story.

Was it his uncle?

Shit yeah, it was, said the Devil. I do my homework, pal. It was a real mother getting that greedy sum' bitch to leave his riches to some poor schmuck nephew he didn't even know he had. But I got him to do it. For what? Chucklehead wouldn't even believe it. Sent him letters, and he threw them all out without reading a word. I mailed all kinds of goodies: winning lottery tickets, vacation packages to Hawaii. Deeds to sports cars. Private freakin' jets, preferred stock in major corporations. Didn't open not one envelope. Chucked everything.

Tried calling him. He didn't answer the phone, erased all his messages without giving them a listen.

I tell you, damn it, I tried everything and the kitchen sink.

118

Got women to come up and hit on him, out of the blue, right in the middle of the street. I'm talking the finest, big-breasted women you ever did see.

Dinkus found a way to muck it up every time. Every single time.

Then I got slick, thought, I'll take the back way into this. Had a rich suit—'nuther Joe on the payroll—had him ram his sports car into the kid's Ma. All the Ma had to pay was a couple bad teeth, was on their way out anyhow, and a few weeks in intensive care. She made millions out of it, and was ready to slide most of that wad on over to her dear old deadbeat. What happened? He didn't visit her once at the hospital. Not once. Said hospitals gave him the willies. Dinkus strikes again. So Ma got good and sore. When she got out the tank, she paid off the house and told the boy, you can rot and die there, for all I care. She bought a mansion up in Edina, sent the boy checks once a month for utilities and food.

Well, at least he was set that way, I said. That's something. He didn't have to work no more.

You know? But no dice, not for this hombre. Kept right on playing his little violin, like I didn't just spruce up his bicycle for him. If you can believe it, Dinkus even starts praying to Big Man.

The Devil raised his hands up high, spreading his fingers out and waiving.

Oh Lord, Lordy Lord, please help me!

Wah wah, woe is me, I sold my soul to the Devil and even he couldn't make this life no better!

But you still had him in your palm, right? I mean, he signed the contract.

I'm telling you, said the Devil, it was like a miracle, only bass ackwards. If I fulfilled even one of his dreams, even one of the dumb ones, he'd have been all mine. No questions asked, no second opinion, bingo, all mine. And if he'd gotten in the way, I mean, if he was trying to stop me from doing my job—I'd still be able to cash in the chips. Show's over, thanks for playing. But there's nothing in the contract that says what happens when the chump was too much of a deadbeat to notice opportunity when it smacked him in the face. I 'spect it's my fault, really. Don't ever trust the lawyers down in Hell, amigo.

But, I said, if he was such a lazy bum, wouldn't you still get him on that? Laziness, that's one the seven bad baddies, ain't it?

Yeah, see now, I thought of that too. But he wasn't lazy, per se. I can't rightly explain it. That's just how he was. It's like, all the lights were on, but nobody was home. Get me? I didn't know what to make of it. Dinkus didn't have much going on, and seems like the rest of the world just couldn't find no useful place to stick him. If he had even done one thing wrong, I would've had him. But no, he played it even the whole time. Not too much to one side or the other.

So what happened? You gave up?

I'm not in the quittin' business, said the Devil.

120

Me, I got forever. That's my ace in the hole. You kids got what, eighty, ninety years? That's nothing to an old timer like me. Heck, I take a walk in the park, whole millennium goes by. Most times, alls I gotta do is sit back and watch. Sooner or later, you all slip up a little, just a little. Then it's say goodnight, Gracie, Bueñas noches. Time to pay the man.

But then, guess what? Out of nowhere, lousy fink has a heart s'plosion and dies. His old man gave him a bum ticker, turned out. Passed it on down from his old man's old man. Whole family had it bad like that. Guess when folks were drawing for body parts, him and his got the short straw.

It wasn't bad food, bad stress, nothing like that. Lucky son of a biscuit was just born with a time bomb wired to his blood box. Wasn't nothing I could do about it.

And he went to Heaven?

Don't know all that, he said. All I know is, I didn't get his soul.

Sounds like a raw deal to me. Seems like you should've had him for something. He had to have broken a rule or two, at some point. Stuck it to his neighbor's wife, backed out of a holy day.

What I'm saying, said the Devil. But I had nada, jack shit to pin on him. I thought to myself, this hombre had to have been up to a something. Maybe Boy Genius was working a sting of his own. Nobody can screw themselves that hard on accident. I start thinking, maybe even Big Man upstairs was in on it, messing with me, trying to pull one over?

That's how I got to thinking. But you know, it don't work like that. Big Man don't have to bother with crap like that. That's all my territory, get me? He don't play dirty like that. Truth is, I just had the bad luck to come across an A-plus flake.

Did you try to take it up with God?

You kidding? Shit yeah. Oh, I sent text messages to Big Man, said the Devil. Texted Big Man like no tomorrow.

Text messages? You talk to God over the phone?

Look, bub, I can't exactly go nancing on up there, now can I, n' ask around for a cup of brown sugar? Long time, no see, amigos. How's the weather up here? Maybe you're a little behind on the story, compadre, but I got myself kicked out of Heaven. Don't take too kindly to me 'round them parts.

Yeah yeah, I said. But I thought the whole punishment was, God won't give you the time of day no more?

Don't know where you heard that malarkey, said the Devil. Me and Big Man, we text all the time. I text Him at least. He don't answer too much. Sometimes I get, *OK* or *GOOD TO GO.* I need to ask Him lots of questions, you know, make sure I'm following protocol. That there's a business word, protocol. I got this small window, you get me. What I can and can't do. Window of opportunity, like. But He keeps on changing the rules. Hard to know what a fella can do anymore.

So I sent Him all kindsa texts, pleading my case, looking for a free pass. Took me a damned lot of texts to get it all out.

You know, they only give you a hundred and sixty characters for every text message. Commas and shit all count. I had to send ten of those, just to get in all the details. What happens? No answer for three months, then He suddenly comes back with *LOL*. I write all that junk, He gives me *LOL*.

I replied back, hell's that supposed to mean, *LOL?* Got the answer right away: *LAUGHING OUT LOUD*. I could see, He was trying to get my goat, so I texted back look, Red Skelton, you're killing me over here. Do I get the soul? Do you get it? Who gets it? What's the score? Four months, no answer. Finally He texted me back: *LMAO*. Had to go ask the fellas about that one. Hardy har har.

I'll tell you what, I'm done texting that comedian. Ho finito. No more. Been doing this job for a mighty long time now, damn long, and lemme tell you, nothing hurts a fella's pride more than knowing that the Creator Himself is out there laughing His ass off at your professional work. That ain't right.

Tough break, I said.

You said it, amigo.

This sort of thing happen a lot to you?

Story of my life, said the Devil. Never had it this bad, but it's a bum deal from the get go. I mean for you mortal folk? It's not a bad setup, you think about it. I put out a nice spread. Okay, here's what I'm bringing to the table: you sign my contract, I make all your dreams come true. Pervert dreams and righteous ones, I got your back.

All I care, you can go and outdo Mother Theresa, you want to.

I'll lead you by the hand the whole way. Two sets of goddamn footprints in the sand, if you get me. Then, when you die, I collect my piece of the eternal pie. That's it. All there is to it. There's the fine print, but that's the gist of it. You get a lifetime of fun, I eventually get a new buddy to hang out with down in the hot tank. Everybody wins.

Until everyone burns in Hell, I said.

Ah, said the Devil. What's Hell anyhow? More'n half of you jokers think you're in Hell already. So what am I doing really? I'm giving you a holiday. A holiday from Hell. The road's long and hard. You don't have to tell me, I know it. What I do is come along and put on the breaks a little, let you coast for a while. Have it your way for a change. And if you ever want out of the deal, you always got the upper hand. All you gotta do is confess your sins, whisper into some beads like you do, dip your head in the holy drink, pray to your hands or whatever the hell. Chances are, Big Man's gonna void the damn contract anyway. What's He gonna do, write you off? Let you sink or swim on your own? Naw, ain't His style. Not how He runs the joint. You people wrote books about this, books out the you-know-what. Big Man, He won't give you your comeuppance if you just say you're sorry, wah wah, you ain't mean it, you're just a low down dirty sinner, oh save me Jesus. All you gotta do. Love you some holy spirit, and you're in. You can live it up on my dime, your whole life, get all your kicks. Then, right before you kick the bucket, you can sign the cross, chat with a holy Joe or somebody, repent your sins and bingo, you skedaddle on up to Heaven, and I'm left here with egg on my face.

124

Tell you the truth, I'm the one who gets the short end.

Must be hard, being you, I said.

You don't know the half of it, amigo.

Well we talked a good long time after that, 'til I had me about four or five more beers in me, half as many whiskey sours.

He wasn't such a bad guy, tell it like it is. Met plenty of worse guys before.

Still, I felt a little, I don't know, queer about it. Something didn't sit right. Couldn't put my finger on it. Didn't know how it was going to go over back at home base.

Martha can't read my thoughts too well when I'm hammered, but even still, just in case, for the drive home I kept trying to think of that one song, fill up my mind, all the way, B-b-b bird bird bird, Bird is the word, well everybody's heard, the bird is the word, b-b-b bird bird bird, over and over (she HATES that song), but when I set foot in the house, Martha was waiting right there, smack in the middle of the living room, with her arms folded and that face that said she knew everything already. It made me sober as all get out. I held up my hands and said hold on, honey, hold on.

I know everything already, she said. But I want to hear you say it and I want to hear you say it NOW.

Alright, I said. I got good news and bad news. I scratched my head. The bad news is, I think I just sold my soul to the Devil. Now wait, just wait a minute, let me get to the good news.

F-ing Bestseller

It's trash bordering on pornography. Of that, there can be no doubt. Normally, I stop reading such novels within the first several pages, but under the circumstances, I was obliged to thoroughly examine it before providing superfluous, diplomatic commentary and approving publication. The company has to maintain the appearance of professionalism, even when it receives an obvious cash cow like the first literary offering by the world's only superhero. That is the one and only excuse for *The House That Love Killt* ever seeing print.

You think the published version is horrible? That's nothing. That's the version that was gone over with a fine-toothed comb by our editing staff. The final draft that we received from Mr. Guy could have been mistaken for any number of languages, English least of all. The best passages showed a rudimentary grasp of grammar and these, quite often, were passages containing wording that had clearly been stolen from pre-existent works. It's not quite plagiarism, since, sadly, the actual characters and ideas are his own creations. But when pages of incoherent, fragmentary babble suddenly smack into a line such as *'...and then, then she knew the face of glory, as his volcanic purple mountain erupted white hot passion lava betwixt her...'* and so on. Honestly. There was a disheartening number of occasions where he misspelled words such as 'which' but then later on would ease into a passage words such as 'betwixt', 'despondent' or 'whilst'—words that I'm not convinced he understands.

But yet, I read all of Amazing Man's—I mean Norm Guy's novel, slowly and carefully, page by maddening page.

After the first chapter, I put away my red pen. After the second chapter I had to confine myself to reading only in the restroom, where there were no writing utensils with which to scribble. About a third of the way in, I just wanted to take a black permanent marker over the whole thing and treat it like a Classified Document suppressed by the CIA. The story—the story!—was about a regular guy, an alcoholic gas station attendant, that's *'fat and tubby and hairy and no good for no nothing'* who somehow still has the time, finance and virility for cocaine binges, sexual deviance and miscellaneous acts of debauchery. This character, skillfully named Nodda Mazin, somehow defies his socially hampering aesthetics to win the sexual favor of every woman he approaches, while still living out a minimum-wage job and *'questioning my stupid place in this big f-ing mess.'* F-ing is my doing, he actually uses the unabridged word. A lot. It is probably the word he uses most, in every way possible: as a verb, a noun, an adverb, an article—even an adjective. In fact, his f-bombs were the most frequent words decorating the novel, along with his near-complete disregard for capitalization and affectation for the adjective 'freakin', i.e. *"and it didn't make no difference cause all them other pretty girlz couldn't get enough of his loving stuff and this girl here was just a freakin' b****face try to bust his gargantuan freakin' frigoles."* Frigoles, I deduced, is similar to the Spanish *frijoles.* It is meant to denote the scrotum. It is also Norm Guy's primary gauge of masculinity—the presence and size of frijoles—which he uses a staggering six hundred and seventy-eight times within the novel. Not that I counted.

Did I mention that several pages of the manuscript were stained? They were, dubiously so.

After adjusting to the revulsion, the 'name the mystery stain' game became a rewarding diversion to reading the actual story. I'll never know for sure, but I think I guessed correctly on a good sixty percent of the stains.

I'm not a sensitive lady. I consider myself fairly liberal. But there must be boundaries. There must be.

Up until then, the worst novel that I had been obligated to read was *Let My Golden Parachute Be Your Golden Shower,* the memoirs of a retired C.E.O. It was six hundred poorly written pages worth of a filthy rich codger's middle-finger salute to the corporate world. Some of the chapters were simply long, un-punctuated rants, and the entirety of it ill-represented a man who spent a large portion of his adulthood earning a seven figure salary. Two chapters literally made me cry. But even that was practically nineteenth century Russian literature compared to *The House That Love Killt.*

When I accepted the task, I did so with anxiety. I'd heard that the great Amazing Man was taking up writing, and I had hoped that all the news reports about him were slanderous, distorted images of an otherwise wholesome individual. In all honesty, I believed that I would end up reading this before bedtime to my son Ricky, who idolizes that sleaze ball. In the end, I completely lost my cool. I went straight to my boss and protested that *The House that Love Killt* would annihilate the company's integrity. We would become the laughing stock of the literary world… That's when I learned that Amazing Man had saved the CEO's daughter from being eaten by a pack of jackals. Basically, Amazing Man could have sent us his unpaid parking tickets and we would have published them.

It isn't a question of whether or not the stupid book is going to get published, said my boss, because the stupid book is *going* to get published. The question is, whether or not *you'll* still be here when it does. He leaned back in his chair and folded his arms. The choice is yours.

The only good that came from the experience? I finally realized that it was time for a career change.

Now, months later, that darned book is everywhere. Throw a rock, and you'll hit a copy. It's selling like hot cakes. The critics all ripped it to shreds, and yet it's flying off the shelves. As I write this, the book is being translated into French, Spanish, German, Japanese and Korean for international release. It isn't because people are dying to discover the immaculate prose of Norm Guy; everyone knows that Norm Guy is Amazing Man, and he didn't win fans based on his charm, wit and strikingly complex grammatical structuring. People just want to see how far down the rabbit hole he goes.

Just look at the inside jacket, at that photo above the bio. He's actually dressed as Amazing Man. No disguise. Sitting by a window. Reading a copy of his own darned book.

My son wanted me to buy him the book, but I said firmly that I would not allow it under my roof. The book may befit a third-grade reading level, but it's only suitable for forty year-old perverts.

I'm only offering this as a warning, in case you're planning a trip to the bookstore to see what the fuss is all about. I'm telling you now: it is smut. It is cringe-worthy smut. It is some of the smuttiest smut I have ever had the displeasure to read.

It's so bad that you'll wonder if the complete absence of respect for proper narrative lucidity was intentional. Another post-modern technique, you'll consider. Sadly, I can refute this, after having both read the manuscript and met the author in person.

Amazing Man was as big as a house. He was dressed in black trousers, a thin button-down shirt that failed to mask the superhero costume underneath (and part of his hairy belly underneath that), a tie and brown construction worker boots. He also wore thick black glasses that contained no lenses. These glasses, I gather, were meant to accentuate his intellect.

I leave you now with a nugget of dialogue from said meeting, to be matched with the contents of the novel which, by all probability, is currently sitting on your book shelf:

This novel here, it gonna be tits. No f-ing bull. Everybody wanna know what's in my freakin' brain alla damn time and here it is right f-ing here. This little baby turd right here gonna be freakin' big, so f-ing big, gonna make me bigger than Billy F-ing Hemingway.

I don't know who Billy Hemingway is. I presume he doesn't exist. I do, however, recall that at one moment during our meeting, whilst Norm Guy pseudo-pitched his great American novel, I espied a small dabble of white powder on his face, betwixt upper lip and mustache. He radiated a pungent mix of odors, predominately whiskey, underarm and roast beef.

Support him if you want. I never will. Jackal or no.

The Box or Whatever

It's under the bed again. The box. Under the bed. And Marguerite's guyfriend Johnny might be dead. I don't know. Maybe he's just unconscious. I hit him with a toaster. Right between the eyes. I hope he's not dead. Even though he's a jerk. I guess you go to jail even for murdering jerks. I don't know if I should call for an ambulance or call the police or text Marguerite. Who first. Marguerite.

My great-grandmother gave me the black box when I was nine. It was Christmas. Everyone got toys and I got sucky clothes. A few sucky dolls, sucky skirts and sucky dresses. My cousins were playing with soldiers and trucks and building blocks and I was supposed to get all dolled up and call it a win. I cried and ran off to hide under the bed in my great grandmother's bedroom. My great-grandma found me and got down on her knees, peeked under the bed and said oh, my treasure, my jewel, what's the matter, don't cry, I saved the best for you.

The gift was a box. A black one. I was to keep it safe and never open it. Inside the box was the end of the world. Open the box, and the world is over. Finished. È finito. What's in the box? I don't know. The end. Of everything. That's what's in the box. My grandmother said to keep it and hide it and never ever open, not for any reason ever. Not unless I wanted everything and everyone to die.

She was a kooky lady, my great-grandmother. Some people said she was full of magic and some people said she was full of crazy. I say six of one, half a dozen of the other. She was fun anyway.

She also used to say that pooping is baking the devil's meatloaf.

I've kept that box all my life. Kept it closed. I haven't really mentioned it to that many people. Never told Dad. Told mom. It ticked her off. Even now, I think she holds it against me. Didn't tell my sister Ramona because she's a bitch. I told my roommates Nina and Marguerite. But now only Marguerite knows. Because Nina's kind of dead.

She's not dead the same way that Marguerite's guyfriend is dead, because more than likely that lousy piece of jerk is going to wake up with a crappy mood and a huge welt on the back of his head. Nope. Nina's the genuine article of dead. Dead dead. Jumped in front of a subway train dead. It's still so hard to think about, even as I write this now. It's hard every minute of every day. Our wolf pack is missing a wolf and we need her so badly, every day. But she's gone.

We still haven't packed up all her stuff. Her mom refuses to come here and even so much as look at any of it. Plus, I think she doesn't want to see me. She hates me, because I have really short hair and read sci-fi books, so in her mind that makes me gay. She's convinced herself that I turned her daughter over to the dark side of the lesbian, and that's why Nina killed herself. Because every woman with short hair is a lesbian, and every lesbian has supernatural mind control powers that can bend the will of any unsuspecting straight girl. Or something like that. Whatever. Anyway, we kept Nina's bedroom door shut. Technically it's Johnny's' room now, but he'd been sleeping on the couch.

He was like, this is stupid, I'll just go and clean it out, this is not a big deal. Marguerite said Hell. No.

Marguerite's freaked out by the idea of walking in there and seeing all the artwork, finished stuff and half-finished stuff and sketches and half-sketches. And as much as Marguerite has changed, we're both agreed that we don't want anyone else touching Nina's stuff. Her sketchbooks. Her pencils and fat markers and thin markers and ink fingerprints everywhere. Fuck.

When Marguerite started hanging out with Johnny Walker, bringing him around the apartment, we all got pissy. He was sucky, and being around him only made Marguerite act sucky too. Nina drew a picture of him and stuck it on the fridge. His name was Mike something, but we called him Johnny Walker because, for some reason, he thought it would be awesome to grow out a pirate mustache and a mullet. Not just a mullet, but a *serious mullet.* I mean it was all serious in the front, all party in the back. Yeah I guess that look could maybe possibly be awesome if you aren't a douche bag, but he was a big-time douche bag. Awesomeness derailed. Nina inked the picture and everything and it looked so freaking good, almost too good for a drawing that's just supposed to poke fun at your best friend's freakish looking guyfriend. Anyway obviously Johnny Walker hated it but he couldn't do anything about it because if he so much as touched the picture he was OUT. That was the rule and everybody knew it. Marguerite is way different now, but she isn't that different.

Yet still, occasionally, when I drank too much I got really nasty and said stuff to piss off Marguerite on purpose, like when I said oh my god, you are such a sellout, you were just waiting for Nina to die so you could go become a soccer mom, only oops you'll never be a mom will you. It was below the belt, too much, cause Marguerite had only told like five people about her operation. I knew I was going too far, but hey, the bourbon said it, not me.

Marguerite works out like crazy these days and she could probably beat the stuffing out of me, or if she wanted she could say something even nastier to make me run crying to my bedroom. And a few times she was nasty, a few times she made me cry and a few times she hit me so hard I literally saw stars. Now, she's smarter than that. She's got her head screwed on right. She knew it was my defense mechanism. She only shook her head and said, you're pathetic.

When I first met Marguerite seven years ago, she had manic panic lime green hair and a lip ring. All her makeup was black. Her dream was to open up a store that was a comic book store, a used book store, a used vinyl store and a coffee shop. All in one. And there would also be an art gallery on the wall. And in a perfect world it would be located next to a bike shop. Or a theater. But only a theater that shows foreign movies. And indie movies. No crappy Hollywood movies.

Marguerite's hair is blond now. Not just blonde— ultra-blonde. Über-blonde. She has this big amazing head full of ultra über-blonde electric currents. And there's a tiny mark under her lip where the ring used to poke out. She doesn't wear black makeup anymore. She wears skirts and white sneakers to work everyday, and keeps her heels in a huge purse that's probably made from the skin of like four whole cows. She has to wear long sleeve shirts and sweaters to cover up all the tattoos.

134

All she does is bitch about her co-workers and talk about restaurants. Only she calls them restos.

If Nina was alive she would say resto, Marguerite, what in the hell is a resto, are you kidding me, your mom's a resto.

For months after Nina died, I thought about opening the box. I'm going to do it, I thought. I'll open the box and end it all and I won't have to feel this way anymore. No more pain, no more hoping that I'll wake up from this awful dream.

I've stared at the box and stared at it hard and had my hands on the box ready to pry it open and then held it really close against my breasts like it might pop open on its own. I kept it in one hand while drinking myself to sleep with the other. I put it in another box then another box then a cardboard box and hid it in the closet, but that didn't work, it made me think about opening it even more. It was best to have it right out in the open, or under the bed next to my shoes. Every morning, I could wake up and reach under the bed and, instead of grabbing my Chucks, grab the box, open it up and finish the whole show.

But instead, instead of finishing the whole show, I mostly laid in bed and thought about Nina. Or Nina and Marguerite, when Marguerite used to be cooler.

It had been Marguerite's idea to move into the city. We'd move into the biggest, cheapest apartment we could find. And we did that, and it was great for like a month, but then I broke up with He Who Shall Not Be Named, or he dumped me rather, and I cut off all my hair and locked myself in my room. Or something like that.

And then when Nina decided she was going to do comics full-time, she stayed in her room most of the time too, with the door closed. I only saw her now and again, in her pajamas, going to get juice from the fridge and leaving ink smudges everywhere.

Marguerite started working for a small label record company; every other weekend these dirty hardcore emo kids would come and sleep in our living room. It got old really quickly. They were all booze hounds and did nothing but yell, scream, smoke up and not flush the toilet. I had to lock myself in my room and even then, I stashed the black box at the bottom of my trash can, sprinkling the top of the can with tampons just to ward off any chump that broke into my room and went around looting. One of those jokers would think it was my stash box, or where I kept my weed, and then the big idiot would open the box and put an end to everything.

Once, I overheard some kid in the living room say, Marguerite, I don't even get it, you're roommate is like for real a hottie, why is she so lame, she is totally like laming her hottiness into an early grave. Like for real, underneath that weird little boy is a like a for-real hot chick and I so don't get what her deal is.

I don't know if he was talking about Nina or me.
Every now and then, after Nina died or whatever, I wanted to say to Marguerite, hey, we should just stay in, order a pizza and read some of Nina's comics. I never said it, but I wanted to. Nina had a ton of comics. Back in that first month, after we moved in, we would have these geek-out parties, just like in the dorms, or on breaks at home when we'd go over to each other's house and spend the whole night reading comics, playing video games and watching movies.

It was like so anti-girly. I remember sometimes at Nina's
house her mom would stumble in reeking of rum. She'd say
something like, what the hell's with you girls? Looks like a
bunch of twelve year old nerdy boys threw up in here. Is that
what y'all wanna be? Twelve year-old boys?

That's just scratching the surface, she'd say more awful stuff
like that until the usually soft-spoken Nina started screaming
go away leave us alone get out get out get out GET OUT

It wasn't a happy home.

Sometimes instead, we'd drive around and go to a diner and
stay there until they kicked us out, drinking coffee and
whatever, reading comics while Nina did sketches right there
on the table. She'd finish like several pages and we'd read it
all right there. She'd hand the pages to us slowly all like, okay
snitches, one coffee stain and I will ink the next page with
your blood.

Nina didn't draw superhero comics. They were all about her,
high school or college and stuff. Sometimes she did comics
about her dreams. Most of it was dark, not really funny. Sad.
But she did say when she got famous she was going to do
Amazing Man comics, just to see what she could come up
with. I couldn't really see that, but whatever. She did do some
funny stuff though. Like a couple of her comics were about
us, the three of us. Only she always gave us weird French
names. She had some comics about how we used to have
pirate night, where we'd sneak a bottle of rum, get wasted
and yell at each other in goofy pirate voices.

It started a while back when we would make fun of my sister's friend from Australia, and the accents got worse and worse until we'd sound like drunken pirates.

There was one hilarious one she did, making fun of that movie about traveling jeans or whatever.

But yeah, most of her comics were dark and depressing. I mean they were totally amazing and everything, I mean seriously, but the stories were kind of always downers.

I really think she could've had a career. And even for a short time Marguerite was on a crusade to make Nina famous; the most she was able to do was get Nina commissioned to do the album art for a couple of hardcore bands that never got big. Then Marguerite got all grouchy cause Nina couldn't pay rent anymore.

Her savings ran out, and for a while she hit up her mom for money. But that ended when it started dipping into Miranda's drinking funds. So Marguerite and I just had to cover her and split the whole rent between the two of us. It also kind of hurt that Marguerite's record label job wasn't turning out the way she thought it would. She thought she was going to end up like the CEO, when really the label just wanted someone with a bachelor's degree to file papers and make the coffee.

Eventually, Marguerite switched jobs to work at a firm as some kind of assistant to the paralegal's assistant. Something like that.

She came home one day with a pair of hundred dollar jeans and a box full of Chai tea and that was that.

I spent a lot of time at my jobs so I didn't have to deal with a lot of the shouting that probably went on. I worked as a barista during the day and a bartender at night, and in between I shut myself in the room and put on music and lay in bed wondering why I was so worthless. Both Nina and Marguerite were masters of their craft. Nina's craft was drawing and Marguerite's craft was being able to walk into a room full of people and totally own it in five minutes. I can't draw for squat, and I kind of don't even really like people most of the time. I'd learn to play an instrument, but I was still doing this thing where I tried not to listen to music, not on purpose anyway, because no matter what song it was, for some lame reason, it made me think of He Who Shall Not Be Named.

He Who Shall Not Be Named was the stinky bearded loser I dated for two stupid years until one day he decided that the only one he could ever commit to was punk rock.

I used to get mad about it, and then really mad, and then even madder. I hated him so much. Then I'd start crying and wonder if I should call him. Then I'd throw the phone at the wall. Take *that,* phone, you're not the boss of me! It would make a loud cracking sound and land of the floor somewhere. Then I'd crawl around the floor to get it, making sure the fucker wasn't cracked. *Then* I'd get back into bed and get in a little more quality crying until it was time to go back to work.

The problem there was that I didn't know how to hide my bad moods at work. That's not so bad at a coffee shop but at a bar, you know, if you can't hide your bad mood you're kind of screwed. I didn't act like an airhead and didn't flirt with the customers so everyone thought I was a bitch.

I was in a pissy mood most of the time and people could always tell, and so they gave me crappy tips which put me in an even pissier mood. Plus since I didn't dress all cutesy and Barbie-ish like the other girls, everyday someone would say something really hurtful and then expect great service afterward. I came in wearing my hoodie one day, cause of the rain, and one of the customers saw me and said oh shit, he's back, it's the Unabomber! When I took off my hood he was like, ah, no hard feelings, man, I'm just fooling around, and he patted me on the back. What hurt was that I honestly couldn't tell if he was still making fun of me or if he honestly thought I was a boy.

I was trying my very best to be nice. I was. Sure I shot everyone evil glances, but, all things considered, they were all lucky. Whenever a guy called me buddy or made a stupid lesbian joke or even looked at me like he might be keeping a smart-alec remark to himself, I was so close to shouting "MOTHERFUCKERS. THAT TEARS IT!" and flipping over tables. Instead, I took their crappy tips and did a lot of swearing in my head. I often cheered myself up by daydreaming, like, imagining how cool it would be if everyone in the bar turned into a zombie, and I had to take them all down with an axe and an Uzi. Wait, that's too easy. A machete and a rifle. Not a rifle. A machete and a forty-five. No. A machete and a bat, and the forty-five is locked up in the safe, and I have to battle my way through a legion of the undead to find the key and shoot my way to salvation. Aim for the head, aim for the head. Playtime's over. Um. Anyway.

It wasn't just me. I wasn't the only one falling apart. We all were.

Maybe Marguerite thought she was okay, climbing the stupid social ladder, but anyone with eyes could see that she was turning into an evil, unstoppable hybrid hipster-yuppie. She was always going to parties and lounges, or out on dates with sleazebags. Sometimes she dated the sleazebags that wear baseball caps backwards and say bro all the time.

Other times, she brought home Mr. Skinnyjeans, and they went off to her room to talk about French movies and boink. Mr. Skinnyjeans is a sleazebag too, he's just better at fooling everybody cause he looks so dang smart, him and those big black glasses of his.

It was like she thought she could bat for the home team and the away team at the same time. What sucked the most was that she was right. Every man on the planet was on a mission to get inside her pants. It was only a matter of which type of cool guy she wanted to hook up with for the night.

Nina was bad too. Okay, in the end she was the worst out of all of us, but I didn't know that at the time. I knew that she was being a misanthrope, which made her one of the gang. I mean, when I hung out with her it was great, but that almost never happened. She was always in her room with the door closed and locked. On the rare occasions when she wasn't in her room, she would sneak out of the apartment without leaving a note or telling anyone where she was going. She'd be gone for hours, without a trace. Where to? Who knows. And she was always vague when we asked her about it later; she would even get pissed off if we were persistent on finding out where she'd been (I don't know! I was just out running a few errands! WHY ARE YOU RIDING ME?!?).

When she finally did come back to the apartment, she'd immediately go back in her room and shut the door. There was no use knocking; she never opened the door for anyone. Maybe she was so into her art that she wasn't aware of the knocking. Most likely, though, she just didn't care. To get her attention, I'd have to call her cell phone and leave a message. Even then, sometimes two days later I'd see her in the kitchen eating cold cereal and she'd be all, oh, sorry I didn't call you back, I've been out of it. I'd try to play it cool, but I was thinking, what are you talking about? Call me back? You live literally twenty feet away from me, you don't have a job and you practically never leave the apartment.

But then, sometimes, we were hermits together. Those were the good times. It didn't happen much, but occasionally Nina let me hang out in her room. I would lay on her bed and read while she drew at her work desk. It wasn't exactly hanging out; we didn't talk much. I read, like, sci-fi novels and stuff, and she drew, and it was like completely silent most of the time. But I don't know, it was still better than being alone. It was comfortable. I guess reading can be a kind of escape, and so can drawing, but although you can escape with that stuff, sometimes it's better to escape with someone there beside you, even if you're each escaping to a different place.

Other times, I wouldn't see her for days or weeks on end, but we kept up with little messages on each other's dry erase board (yes we still used dry erase boards like a bunch of college kids; SO WHAT???). We both had really vivid dreams, you know, like powerful ones.

142

But really random words and phrases would pop up in our dreams. We made up this game, to try really hard to remember them and then go write them on the other person's dry erase board as soon as possible the next morning. So I wouldn't even see her for days but then one morning LOBOTOMY HANDJOB would magically appear in big bubble letters on my board. Or I would get out of bed one morning and keep repeating to myself TURKEY McTURKISH, TURKEY McTURKISH over and over until I made it to Nina's door to scribble it on her board.

It was way better than a real conversation. It's so boring to hear people talk about politics or books or movies or how drunk they got last weekend, but I think it says a lot when someone wakes up one morning with the words FINNEGAN'S NIPPLE still floating around in her head, fresh out of her subconscious, and the first thing she wants to do is go and tell you about it.

Only then one morning, she wrote TRAIN TO CATCH. L8RZ on my dry erase board. When I read it, I thought, she's slipping, that's a boring one. It took almost the whole day before I realized that it was the closest thing to a suicide letter that Nina had left.

Then… after that, like every day I wanted to open the box. It was the first time. I had a strong urge to do it. Before that, before Nina died, I never wanted to open it. Never. I was the Great Protector. Guarding the box, keeping it shut—that was my Duty. Even when I was mad or sad, when I looked at the box I always felt better. As long as I kept the box, safe and closed, everything was okay. But then, with Nina gone, I just didn't see the point. It was all hopeless.

I looked at the box and a voice inside me whispered, *do it, just do it, it wouldn't be hard, not as hard as what she did.*

I taped a photo of Nina on the lid of the box. That helped. I first showed the box to Marguerite and Nina back in college. We were hanging out in my dorm room one night (Marguerite and I were roommates, that's how I met them, in college; she and Nina had been friends since kindergarten). Marguerite's boyfriend and some other guy were there. We were all wasted and laughing or whatever, and in the middle of it all I took the box out from the green milk crate under my bed.

I told them everything. I told them stuff about my great-grandmother, how she knew all this crazy gypsy magic and way back in the day she put a curse on one guy and like a month later he exploded into a pile of sand. I told them about the photo album that my uncle had, with photos and newspaper clippings about people that my great-grandmother cursed. The next time I saw him, I was going to ask my uncle if I could borrow the album so that I could make copies of everything. It was awesome, even if some of it was kind of disturbing. Like even too disturbing for me. The creepiest was what happened to—oh man—this guy driving the bus that killed my great-grandmother. I guess she cursed him right before she died, and two months later he was hit by a station wagon. Like, for serious, he was in a store and a station wagon came flying out of nowhere and crashed right into him. Wild.

Dude, said Marguerite's boyfriend Jason Jungles, this is nuts. Marguerite, he said, when you told me that your roommate was way cool, you left out the part where she's also totally mental. What happened next was awesome. Marguerite wasn't even facing him.

144

Her back was turned facing the bookshelf and CD tower on the far wall. She spun a full hundred and eighty degrees and head-butted him. It was perfect, and fluid, like, how did she even know exactly where he was in the room, to turn right to him and deal a head-butt? Jason dropped to the floor. His nose started bleeding. Silence.

Okay said Marguerite, the penis to vagina ratio in this room is totally throwing off the feng shui. If you have a penis, get the fuck out. Now.

Jason and the other guy left without saying a word.

That's how badass Marguerite used to be.

Afterward she was all 'so anyway, Giulia, you were saying...?' Like that, like she hadn't just beat up her boyfriend seconds ago. I realized that she was being for real; she really did want me to keep on talking, so I told them more about my great-grandma's gypsy curses. Then I told her about Christmas and how I got the box and how my mother was really bitter to me for a long time because she was jealous that great-grandma didn't give her the box. Marguerite and Nina both listened closely and asked lots of questions, but Nina was paying the most attention. She was like hanging on my every word, and when I finished, she looked me in the eye and said you can never open that box. I said yes, I know and she said no really, you can't. I nodded and she said no, really, don't do it, no matter what. It kind of creeped me out. The box, it was important to me, but it was also like a game. The look on Nina's face, though...she was, like, not joking even a little. She was dead serious, more serious than I ever was about it.

She was probably just high, but it was way convincing at the time. You're the luckiest person in the world, she said. Then she hugged me and kissed me on the cheek.

I started taking it around with me. In my book bag. The box, I mean. A month or so after the funeral, I took it around everywhere. Sometimes in the morning, I'd set it in front of me on the kitchen table and just stare at it while I drank my coffee. There it is. Right there. Death for everybody. Everything. I took it out of the apartment too, on the train, on my bike. At the bar I'd keep it under the counter as I worked, on the floor in my bag. At any moment, someone could've gone into my bag, took it for a box of tea or something, opened it up and screwed us all.

At home, lying in bed with the lights out, staring up at the ceiling, holding the box against my breasts. In the other room, I could hear Marguerite having sex with whoever it was this time. Sometimes I'd cry, sometimes I would just lay there and think stuff like, man, it would be so much cooler if I knew for sure that Nina was in her room drawing.

One time, in the middle of the night, I came out of the bedroom to get something to eat and there Marguerite was, sitting at the kitchen table, in her jammies, staring at the ground, glass of wine on the table. She looked spent. I didn't want to say anything, but I was probably saying way too much by being silent.

I know what you think she said, slurring her words and staring at the ground. You think I'm a sellout. She thought I was a sellout. Everyone thinks I'm a sellout now. Well fuck you guys.

I didn't call you a sellout, I said, trying to ease out, but it was too late. Marguerite was drunk and out for blood. Plus, she was kind of right, that's exactly what I'd said.

You don't know nothing, she said, you think you're so cool but you're not. You weren't even her better friend. You just think you were. Ha. I known her since forever. Where were you when we was in high school? I had to stick up for her every week. Where were you, when everybody was laughing and calling us the dyke twins? I saved her butt so many times it's not even funny. I almost got curbed-stomped, fighting some dudebros that was gonnsta rip up her sketchbook. I'm the momma in this house. I been the momma for years and years and years. You're the sellout. I'm the momma.

I didn't say anything, and slowly backed away.

Pretty soon after that, Johnny Walker started living at our apartment. He was sleeping on the living room couch, but Marguerite promised him Nina's room as soon as we could clear everything out. So far, we were planning to do that around the twelfth of Never.

Johnny was a total roach though. He didn't have a job, and all he ever did was walk around the apartment in his boxers, eating cold cereal and chugging beer. He left beer bottles and cereal bowls all over the place. I hated it. I wasn't really okay with a guy living in our apartment in the first place, but we needed the rent money, and I couldn't say much because Marguerite was paying more of the rent than I was. Plus Johnny was the backup attachment guy when Marguerite was looking to get laid but didn't want to leave the apartment. Technically they were dating.

147

They weren't faithful, or even cute and lovey-dovey. But because they boinked every now and then, Johnny thought it crowned him king of the house. He would go strutting around like Mr. Big Time.

But then, he went too far.

It was morning. I was in the kitchen, at the table, drinking my coffee and staring at the box. He walked in wearing boxers and nothing else. He was like, what is this thing? He lifted the box right off the table.

Give it back! I surprised myself by how high my voice shot up.

Calm down, said Johnny. So this is your doomsday device? Ha ha. So gay. Marguerite said you were a little flake.

I reached for the box, but he pushed me back with one hand. I was pissed, but also a little scared at how much stronger he was.

If you don't give it back, I hissed, you will so regret it.

He said something sarcastic, but I was so mad that I couldn't even hear straight. He took the box with both hands and smirked at me, making a fake-out motion like he was going to open it up. I don't even see what the big deal is he said, this is like some kind of kid's—

He didn't finish. I ran to the kitchen counter and grabbed the closest heavy object I could get my hands on—the toaster.

I yanked the cord out of the wall, grabbed the toaster with both hands and heaved it at Johnny as hard as I could. It smacked him right in the face. He fell to the floor. The box fell with him. I snatched up the box and ran off to my room. I slipped the box back under my bed. That's where it is now. Where it should be.

I sat at the kitchen table to finish my coffee. I texted Marguerite:

ur dude touched my box. threw the toaster at his head.
i might have killed him. ha ha thats a haiku.

Let me tell you about one other night when the three of us all hung out. It was in college. I was goofing around on the computer and Marguerite was lying in bed studying statistics, and Nina knocked on our door and came in all wide-eyed and so obviously tripping. She was like, oh my god you guys, we so need to go drive around and howl at the moon. Wait I said, is that, like, code for something? I didn't get the memo. No said Nina I mean like drive around, look at the moon and totally howl at it. Doesn't that sound perfect? I didn't know what to say to that, and just stared at her, then looked over at Marguerite like, um...? Marguerite didn't miss a beat. She closed her book, got up out of bed and was all, let's do this. And so we drove around until almost two in the morning on a Thursday night. Nina stuck her head out of the passenger seat window and howled at the moon. She did all the howling, Marguerite and I didn't join in, although every once in a while Nina would poke her head back into the car to say come on, you guys have to try this, it's the best. We did not. She howled and howled and then passed out on the passenger seat.

On the drive back to the dorm, Marguerite told me that if we didn't play along, Nina probably would have run off and hurt herself. She didn't say exactly what Nina would have done, and I didn't ask. Anyway, she said, if I want to do something screwed up like this one day, you better have my back. I didn't answer and she said I am not joking. If I ever go batshit crazy, you better be there, drinking the Kool-Aid right along with me. I mean it. Promise. Or go to hell.

I promised.

Marguerite came into the room. There in the kitchen. Me, coffee, coffee table. Spilled bowl of cereal, dude in boxers on the floor. Toaster.

Is there any more coffee, asked Marguerite. She poured herself a cup.

Is he dead?

I shrugged.

Don't know. Maybe not?

Did he open the box?

We're still here, I said. So no.

Marguerite sat down at the table, next to me.

And where is here?

Sipped coffee.

Sometimes, she said, I think you opened that box a long time ago.

I didn't answer. Silence.

Marguerite said, you know what Nina would say, if she was here.

Yeah, I said. I do.

Lousy Stinking Elixir of Love

I bought the love potion on Tuesday evening, on the way
home from the office. I slipped it into Jane's earl gray tea,
just after dinner, during that little grace period in between
prime time television and the evening bitch-out. She went
off to the bathroom and I dumped the whole mother load
into her mug. It was supposed to be tasteless. The tea is
called Han Sarang tea. I bought it at a stuffy little shop in
the Korean neighborhood ten minutes northeast of our condo.

On Thursday night, Jane said that marrying me was the worst
mistake she ever made ever.

On Friday morning, she left to go stay with her sisters in
Macomb.

My first impulse was, I'll sue. Call the police. I'll do
something. The hammer of justice must strike. Luckily,
before putting any crazy scheme into action, I came to my
senses and recognized that it might not be a wise decision to
go and inform the authorities that I'd attempted to drug my
wife. Instead, I returned to the shop, receipt clenched between
my fist. Maybe I just wanted an apology? I didn't really
expect a refund. Honestly, I didn't even want my lousy
hundred dollars back. I sure as hellfire didn't want another
vial of that worthless juice. It was about piece of mind. You
can't go around screwing people over with that Asian hoodoo.
You have to at least throw out a bone every now and then.
Even a really small bone will do. I bought the potion
thinking, what am I doing, what am I doing, what am I,
some kind of moron?

And yet I thought okay, look, even if all it means is she wants to spoon in bed once in a while, I'll consider it a success. That will do. It seemed to me that periodic spooning was the bare minimum of what I could expect from a love potion. I was prepared to set the bar that low.

I didn't get periodic spooning. I got a letter that didn't have my name on it and said *I'd rather spend the rest of my life with my sisters and that stinking German Shepherd. I'd rather go back and stay with Dad, stinking booze hound that he is, than spend another day in this stinking place with you.*

The owner of the store was a round, bespectacled guy named Dr. Gong. His English was pretty good. He was extremely well-dressed, suit and tie, sharper than the average shop owner, maybe even too sharp for a shop as shabby and cluttered as his. He wore thick glasses and a big, jolly smile, the latter of which disappeared the instant he sat down behind his tiny office desk and took a good look at me.

I was probably a little, no very rude; without any greeting or warning, I launched right into it, and by the end of it I was raising my voice and telling him that his lousy crap killed my lousy marriage. When I was done, I'd gotten all red in the face, panting. Doctor Gong just stared at me blinking for a few moments, without expression, then sighed and mumbled under his breath what I assumed was an insult in Korean. Then he said, it is always the same, with you people. I asked him what the heck that meant and he said, you are in my store. You see that I have potions. Potions everywhere. Look at any wall, you will see potions. So many potions. But you people come and you take the love potion.

That set me off, and I was already itching for a reason to shout.

What the hell, I said, was I supposed to buy the damned migraine potion? I wanted more damned love in my marriage, so I bought the damned love potion. He shook his head.

I have a sex potion. Anyone who drinks it will have a lust. Very strong. You will need sex, with anyone. Maybe it does not matter who. I have a friendship potion. I have three or four hate potions. I have a potion to feel like young man. A potion to be inspired. A potion to feel smart, even if you are stupid. I have a fertility potion, and a potion for wanting a baby. These two, they come in a set. I have a potion to pretend so you are gay, and a potion to pretend so you are not gay. I have one potion, if you make someone drink it, they will stay with you forever. Always. No matter what, they will stay next to you. I have these. I have a potion for so many a thing. But you people, you come and you ask for the love potion. Always the love potion. You ask and I give and you do not become happy.

I'm not going to listen to this bull—I don't want to be smart. I don't want inspiration. I don't want to be gay. All I wanted is for my damned—all I wanted is for my wife to love me again, like she used to. That's it. That's what I paid for.

Doctor Gong leaned back in his chair, folded his arms.

My potions work. One hundred percent. If you buy my potion, if you think my potion is not working, this means that you have bought the wrong potion. But the potion is not wrong. You are wrong.

It was no use arguing anymore. My heart was racing and I wanted to yell, but I didn't. Yelling when I wanted to cry was part of what got me into this mess in the first place. So I just stood up, shrugged and said well, what the heck, can you recommend anything now?

Doctor Gong said, after a notably long pause, one time ago, one man was very smart. Very smart man. This man asks for a potion that will make him think so the world is not trying to ruin him. I have a potion like this. It is not expensive. But he is the only one who asks for this potion.

I'll take eight ounces of that one then, I said.

No, said Doctor Gong. You go home. I will sell you nothing today. Go home. Think. Right now, you do not think. Maybe, you want the world to ruin you? Many people want this. If you must come back, come back after one week. Two weeks. Go home now. Think. You want your wife to love you more. If she drank my potion, she is this way. Guaranteed. My potion has worked. Be happy.

I went home.

I hear from Jane a few times a month. Sometimes she calls about something trivial, something she forgot to pack up. Sometimes it's a bill that has to be switched over to my name. Or mail forwarded. Sometimes, she calls and I'm not sure why and before I know it she's screaming at me and bringing up every little thing she's ever held against me and every other word is stinking, because she uses that word the same way other people use actual profanity.

It's stinking that and stinking this and I can't get a single word in; when I even try to interrupt her she shouts some stinking something into the phone and hangs up.

And then even when we're being cordial, she still sounds hateful and malicious in an offhanded way, like, I am soooo glad that we never had any kids, can you imagine? Or boy, we were so terrible together, can you imagine? Always asking me to imagine it, as if, with all the things to imagine, I wanted to imagine the unlimited possibilities in a dysfunctional marriage. No thanks.

But still she calls. Shouting and screaming, she calls. For big reasons and little reasons, she calls. It has been four years now and the only thing I have ever been able to count on is her eventual phone call. In another four years, she will still find reasons to call. In another forty years—God help us, should we live so long—if people even still use phones by then, she will find reasons to call.

Unless, of course, a much bigger reason gets in the way. I can only think of one such reason, and there's probably no potion to let you sneak away from it.

I don't know how all that sounds to you. Maybe it sounds like Hell. Maybe it sounds comforting. Anyway, it's something to think about if you ever go looking to buy the lousy stinking elixir of love.

A Special Thing

The one and only thing that I can say with certainty is that I hate cigarettes. Cigarettes are disgusting. I don't like them now, I have never liked them, and I never will. Practically everybody else at the Nights is a chain smoker. More than once I've thought, why not, it'll give me a reason to take a break every hour and a half. But no. No way. I'm happy to say that I can't stand cigarettes. Not the taste of them and not the smell. Not the way the smoke gets into your clothes and your hair and all over your hands. Cigarettes are disgusting.

This is probably going to sound superficial, but that's probably the most important self-discovery I've ever made. I feel like such a loser writing that. But it's the truth.

I went to a psychic reader on my twenty-fifth birthday. I don't believe in that stuff, so I don't really know why I went. All right. I don't not believe in fortune telling. Who knows what I believe anymore. I don't think I believe in God, but what do I know? Lots of people believe in God, or Allah—something. Plenty of those people are smarter than I am. So I could be wrong. I'm probably wrong. Don't really care. But psychics, I was pretty sure that was a load of baloney, like, a certified load of baloney; not like the God thing, which is a contestable load of baloney. It all just comes down to boredom though. A cure for boredom trumps all.

I admit it, though, I was a little curious about it too. I'm a sucker for all of that stuff: psychics, ghosts, aliens, the occult. Buddy, my old co-worker at the Nights, was way into stuff like that. Aliens especially. If you wanted to know about aliens, Buddy was the nerd to talk to. He was the alien guy.

I had a hard time believing all of it myself, but it's still really fascinating.

I wonder what happened to Buddy. He quit the Nights about a year ago. Just stopped showing up. We were pals, hung out at work three times a week. Then, he up and quit. Poof. Gone. None of us hang out outside of work, so no one had his number. Delete, delete, delete. Either we deleted him, or he deleted us…but now, he's definitely gone. Anyway…

Anyway, I had other reasons for going to the psychic. I guess… I was pretty lonely around then. I'd just lost my best friend. My best friend Angie flew away to Europe.

I'm writing about it now, because, more recently, I lost another friend: a kid I used to know way back in elementary school. He drove his station wagon into a quarry. I should be thinking about him, grieving and such, but honestly, it just made me think more about Angie.

Angie and I used to hang out at this comic book store all the time, just swinging on the flippity-flop (sorry, inside joke). Angie 'worked' there (if you call that work), while I loitered. It basically amounted to the same thing though; I covered her plenty of times when she had to go run errands. I just didn't get paid for it. I guess it balanced itself out, since I read an f-ton of comics that I didn't have to pay for. Even on top of that, it was great to just sit around and talk. Angie wasn't like a typical, you know, girly girl. I don't want to get all stereotypish, but I think there are really two main kinds of girls out there: girls who think that screaming, exploding heads are awesome… and the rest. Angie was in the former category. The rest, eh, I don't care for them.

She didn't talk about her hair or shopping or anything; she wore the same two knit hats all the time. That was her thing. No matter what time of the year, knit hat. It kind of made her look boyish, but she didn't care. That made it even cooler, that she seriously didn't care if people didn't think she looked womanly enough. Whatever that means. And I swear, she had more tattoos than anybody. Like, except for working at comic book stores and record shops, she was practically unemployable.

Once, she almost got me to get a tattoo.

We went over to Blud Paint Tattoos, where she got all of her ink. But the owner, her friend, took one look at me and got really angry. Angie, who told you to bring this poser in here, he said. He wasn't Jewish, but his wife was. Just my dumb luck. Apparently he'd been studying Judaism for months, and had been considering converting. He thought I was making a mockery of it by the way that I dressed. Angie, he said, you know I love you like my little niece. I'd work on every inch of your body if you asked me to. But don't you ever bring this jack-off here again.

I tried to defend myself. He interrupted me mid-sentence. No. No. Shut up. You think you're a Hasidic Jew, just cause you put on that hat? You're not. You're a jack-off. I said shut up. Stop talking, jack-off, before I throw you out of that window. And then I'm going to kick your ass, because replacing the window is going to cost me money I ain't got. Hey. I said shut up. I don't want to hear your fucking poser mouth. You probably want to say something in Yiddish just to be a little twat. Get out of my shop.

That was my first and last tattoo experience.

Tattoos aside, Angie and I could talk about everything. I mean everything. Not just comics, not just music, not just deep life stuff. Everything. Sometimes we talked about making a comic together, although neither one of us could draw. Then for a while we were going to make a zine, just the two of us. The comic store gets a ton of them every week. We'd read through them, compare, talk about how our zine would look. Our zine was going to be called Busted Tires and oh how awesome was it going to be. It was going to be about bikes and bands and how stupid life is.

We never did any actual work on Busted Tires, but that's beside the point. Talking about it was way more fun than making it would have been. Also, less work.

What else can I say about Angie? She's like the only person that didn't make fun of me for dressing like a Hasidic Jew. Even my mom made fun of me about it. The first time she saw me with my new clothes, she was like, aw hell. Here we go again. Now my son thinks he's some kind of half-assed Rabbi. What next?

Angie was different. All she said was, that hat is effing badass. Dude. Today's Switch Hat Day. Here, let's switch hats.

No way, I said, I don't want your janky hat. You never take off that hot mess. You probably wear it to bed.
It's so grody.

Whatever, she said. Then she said YOINK! and swiped the fedora right off my head.

160

Hey, I said. Give that back before I break you.

Make me, she said, teasing me with it. All right, I said, if that's the way you want it, woman—taste the black sperm of my vengeance!

So, ah, yeah. We spent a lot of time getting wasted and beating each other up for fun. We seriously beat each other up, punching and kicking until both our noses were bloody and we were on the floor wheezing and laughing at the same time. It was like a fight club, only not. Yes, it was a game. Yes, we were kidding around, But at the same time, we were causing each other very real, no shit pain.

But then, she suddenly took off. Well, not suddenly. She was nearly hit by a bus. It caused this big spiritual awakening for her. Ugh. She got all weird and philosophical, like, always wanting to have deep conversations. She stopped watching movies altogether and started saying that most of the comics we both used to like were 'trite'. Before that, I'm sure I never heard her use that word before.

Then she became obsessed with the guy who saved her. Stupid me actually helped; my uncle's a cop, if you can still call them cops when they sit behind desks all day. I got him to pull some strings and get all the dirt on her great amazing savior. But then it turned out that her great amazing savior was this totally scummy dude who, like, beat women and molested little boys.

Even still, Angie kept a picture of the loser, framed it, and talked about him all the time. She talked about him like the guy was Jesus. It was really freaking mental.

161

Then, completely out of the blue, she decided to quit her job, pack her stuff and fly to Iceland.

Twenty-six years with her aunt, and just like that, she was ready to disappear. The only real explanation she gave me was a text message that read:

don't wanna work no more. gonna quit my job and be a crusty.

I thought she was kidding.

She wasn't.

She bought a passport and a one-way ticket. I think she must've spent all the money she had in the world just on that. She said that she was going to sleep wherever until she figured out what to do next.

It ruined the whole friendship. I got ticked off. What about me? What am I supposed to do? And she was all, you could come with. Oh, I see, I said. Super, let me liquidate some of my assets and get back to you. Have you lost your ever-loving mind? Europe? I don't even have gas money for my mom's stupid crappy Subaru.

We got into a huge argument. I said a bunch of mean things. And ridiculous things. I called her a traitor. Thanks a lot, I said, you selfish traitor. You... you Benedict Arnold of friends!

I don't know where that came from. Benedict Arnold of friends? What does that even mean? Sometimes I say things like that out of nowhere.

When I said it, Angie started laughing. On another day it would've made me laugh too. We would've spent the rest of the night joking about it.

It would've been our inside joke for months. Benedict Arnold of friends. You can't make that stuff up.

But I was too angry to realize how goofy I was being. I shouted into the phone, literally shouted, fine! Go on and laugh! Laugh all the fucking way to Europe! Just forget about me. Fucking forget we were friends. I don't ever want to talk to you again. Ever.

She stopped laughing. Dead silence. I hung up the phone.

That was the last time I talked to her. Maybe it's the last time I'll ever talk to her. I erased her number from my phone, blocked her email address from my account, deleted all the old emails. Delete, delete, delete. I did it all in this big pissed-off rush, like I was doing it all out of spite, in case the Future Me ever wanted to make amends. Maybe she could've still found a way to get in touch with me, if she wanted to. She didn't. By now, she's probably living in Europe. I'm sure everything's so exciting and new over there that she think about me anymore. She's probably met some Spanish guy named Javier, who has an earring and a permanent five-o'clock shadow. He probably likes the taste of her sweat. Something gross like that. But even so, if I ever met him, I bet I'd be incapable of hating him. His coolness would be so mighty that I would probably turn all-the-way gay for him.

I miss Angie. A lot.

I did have other friends, kind of—but not really. There were the guys at the banquet hall, but they don't really count. It says everything that I usually think of them as 'the guys at the banquet hall' and not as 'my friends at work'. And the rest were just internet friends. That made them almost not even real people. That sounds mean. But I bet everyone feels that way now.

Around the time when everything went down with Angie, I stopped using the internet. Ha. I know, right? Oh goodness, that's crazy, how could anyone ever live without the sacred internet? All right, I used it, yes, a little, but not to talk to anyone. I didn't want to use it as my social network. Social network, that's such a crock. What the internet is ideal for is shutting people out, not getting closer to them. You can build this universe full of 'friends', but then whenever you want, you can totally shut out everyone and no one will say anything about it. It's sad and so wrong, but also relieving. Delete, delete, delete. Block and disappear.

Still, part of me still expected to get a bunch of random messages. *"Where are you?" "WTF?" "Earth to Marius—what's up?"* Nope. I got nothing. Everyone just silently moved on. I don't like thinking about it, really. It makes me think of how Nick probably felt. At the end.

I guess that also, things just stopped feeling… permanent. Except for a few people, I didn't talk to any of my old high school friends. There was just Angie, and I thought we would always be friends. We were almost like brother and sister. But then after one phone call, we were nothing. Strangers. Then, when I heard about Nick (I read about it in the paper, that's how I found out; can you believe that?

A stupid newspaper!), and that came waaay the hell out of left field.

I don't remember talking to him beyond the fifth grade, and I never really had a reason to think about him again. Until I found out that he was dead.

Teenage suicide, five years after he stopped being a teenager.

It made me look back and see that basically, nobody is permanent. Just friends for now. Coming and going. Maybe not even friends; just people who would be chummy for a little while, then go away. Even if they weren't going to go away, sooner or later they'd die.

It made me want to be alone. All the time.

The psychic reading place was way in the city. I hate driving out to the city. Every driver in the city is a total dick. I'm included: just being in the city makes me act like a dick too. It's hard not to be a dick. The air is dirty and smoky. The streets are all congested and loud. It takes almost two hours to drive like ten miles. And then, when you finally get out of the car and pay the meter ten bucks for two stupid hours, you get harassed by bums. Bums and crusty college kids. All begging for money, even though they all live in the city and probably make twice what I make serving roast beef and mashed potatoes to smelly old war vets. And the city has bars and porn shops everywhere; generic coffee shops and hipsters acting like the cat's pajamas. The city is just ginormous and grody. Not like the burbs are any better— there's nothing to do in the suburbs except to die slowly from boredom—but at least it's not a crazy bum parade.

But I had to go into the city for my psychic reading. There aren't any psychic reading places in the burbs. They aren't practical, and if the suburbs are about anything, it's looking sensible. And I mean looking practical. The burbs are just as backwards and fucky as any other place, but they try so hard to look practical. That's the main thing.

The place was on the second floor in this old building on the south side. Pretty easy to miss; it was just a neon green marquee hanging in front of a window: Psychic Readings. A little neon white hand pointing upward. I didn't understand that part. What does that hand even have to do with anything? In general, I saw a lot of those places whenever I went in the city—which was less and less often over the years as I slowly stopped coming out here to visit friends (mostly because all of them got infected with that virus that makes people pair up and start breeding for no good reason). Every time I passed a psychic reading place, I thought it seemed like such a scam, but a mysterious one. There had to be something to them, or they would be illegal. But what? You know? I didn't get it. You'd think psychic readings would be illegal if they were a total con. Right? If they were complete lies, like, "hey buddy, let me sell you the Brooklyn Bridge," then someone would have put a stop to them. Somebody. I would think.

There was always that question mark. What was it like?

I thought about the psychic reading all day at work, on my birthday. I had to be extra careful, because I thought I was going to be so side-tracked thinking about my birthday present that I was going to drop plates and spill water on old people all evening.

I got excited about it, though. Got more excited as the day went on. I didn't really know what to expect.

Would the psychic wear, like, a turban? Would there be a crystal ball? Would I hear crazy stuff, or just whatever I wanted to hear? "You're going to meet the woman of your dreams!" "You're going to get a great job and a house and blah blah blah!" Or would I hear something seriously fucky?

"Oh my, it's almost too horrible to say, you're going to die in seven days!" Or maybe even, would it be like the horoscopes, where the psychic says just enough for you believe whatever you want? You know: "Luck will soon find you, even if you don't realize it." I thought it might also, maybe, be one of those traps where the psychic is just really perceptive. You walk into the room and immediately the psychic sizes you up and sees all these little details about you. From that, they can figure everything out. Every tiny detail. And that's how they know what your 'fortune' will be. Bleh.

Or maybe I was wrong?

When the fish fry was finally over, I went home really quick, showered, changed clothes (cause I reeked of catfish and mostaciolli) and took the Subaru into the city.

After spending a whole stupid hour just to find a parking space, I made it to the building and went up a flight of stairs into the Psychic Reading place. It was really regular looking. Like, nothing about it looked very spooky or psychic-ish. It looked like somebody's dingy apartment. No bead curtains or anything. There was this waiting area with a ratty orange carpet; it looked like the 70's threw up all over the floor.

167

It led into to what was clearly a living room, with some old guy on a recliner, watching TV.

The psychic was an older-looking lady, I don't know, forty-five or fifty or so. Heavy set, big hair.

Almost fake-looking hair. Like a big poofy hair helmet.

I was only sitting in the waiting room for a couple minutes before she came in and got me.

She was wearing a yellow flower print muu muu. Bare feet. She smiled and, without saying anything, led me into the 'psychic chamber'.

The psychic room was their grody dining room with the lights dimmed. We sat on opposite sides of a card table covered with a white tablecloth. There was a yellow candle planted in the middle of the table. That was supposed to make everything look spooky and magical.

The psychic lady winked at me. I like your style, kid, she said. I couldn't tell if she was making fun of me. She didn't look like she was teasing. Thank you, I said, with a little hesitation. She reached out to pat me on the shoulder softly. I mean it, she said. You're a good, clean boy. Don't see that so much no more. How's that working out for you?

How's what working, I asked. She just gestured towards me with both hands.

This whole thing you got going on here. How's it going?

Not so well, I said. Everyone thinks I'm trying to look like a Hasidic Jew.

You are though, right? She said. She said it so plainly that it took me off guard.

I guess so, I said.

Nothing wrong with that, sweetie. S'like all I see anymore are little boogers tryin' to look like rap stars, their pants alla way down to their ankles. You wanna look like a Hasidic Jew? Good for you. It's a spiffy look.

Puff. Cloud of smoke.

Oh, and don't you believe that couch stinker, she said abruptly, pointing her cigarette right at me.

Who…?

She pointed her cigarette towards the door leading to the living room.

My husband, that's who. He's always drunk. Don't listen to nothing he says.

But he didn't tell me anything, I said. She shook her head, popped the cigarette back between her lips. There must be an art to smoking like that; she'd mastered it.

Move someplace warm. San Francisco. They got good vibrations in San Francisco. New Mexico. Anyplace, I don't care. But he's stuck on this town. Beats the heck out of me.

He will. When he does, don't pay no attention to him, sweetie. He just drank his weight in scotch.

Let him start talking and he'll tell you who started the Chicago fire. Don't pay him no mind.

Puff. Cloud.

So, she said, what brings you here? I started to answer, and she giggled and raised a hand to stop me. I'm just yanking your ding-a-ling, honey. Of course I know why you're here, Marius.

She knew my name. That was legitimately freaky.

Don't worry, she said. It's okay. I know, it's spooky, oooh, the psychic is really psychic. But I promise you, It's okay. Girl Scout's honor. Now let's get down to brass tacks, shall we? You want to know your future. Give me your hands.

I gave her my hands. She held each one with both of her hands, firmly, her fingers pressing into the palms, then feeling the backside. Softly, then rough. Nobody, especially a girl, really ever touched me like that.

Relax, she said. Don't get all worked up. This ain't no Thai massage, sweetie.

She pressed my hands more. Her long, painted nails stabbed into my palm. It kind of hurt. Cold out there, isn't it, she said. I nodded. Around February every year, I tell Francis—that's my better half, Francis. Half of what? Your guess is as good as mine. I tell Francis: We need to get the heck of out Dodge.

It's not a bad city, I said. I like it. She didn't respond. Pressed my hand a bit more.

So, she said, finally letting go of my hands, what do you wanna know?

I didn't know how to answer. Mouth half-open. She started chuckling.

Still yanking, sweetie. Never gets old, I swear. I'm sorry, I can't help it.

What can I say, it's a lot funnier over on this side. She smiled. It was a very sweet smile.

You're gonna be just fine.

What do you mean?

She shrugged.

You're gonna be okay. Things are gonna be okay for you.

Just okay?

Yeah. You don't have nothing to worry about.

It wasn't what I expected to hear. Would I win the lottery? Meet the girl of my dreams?

Eh. It'll be decent.

What does that mean?

Figure out what to do with my life?

I don't know what to tell you, she said. You're gonna live
an alright life. Nothing much is gonna happen, yadda yadda
yadda, then you get cancer and take the long journey to the
Great Beyond, as Babcia used to say. God rest her soul.

Cancer?

Yeah. It's in your genes. Eh, that's how people die these days.
It's really nothing to get worked up over. Sure, it's gonna hurt
a little at the end. But heck, you got a good fifty years ahead
of you before it turns into a big thing. The good news is, you
can smoke all you want; it won't make no difference. You
don't smoke now, right? You ought to start. It's nice, something to do with your hands.

When you leave, do yourself a favor, go buy yourself a pack
of menthols. I'd offer you one of mine, but trust me, they're
not your style. Ultra-lights. You'd hate the taste and never
want to smoke again.

I was at a loss. I stammered around for a good question.

Do I get married?

Yeah, she said.

And… ?

And what?

How is it? I'd like to know about it.

I mean you won't go bragging about it, but it won't be terrible. Good enough to get by on.

That's it?

That's what I see.

Well... does anything really big, exciting happen to me?

She shrugged. Kid, seriously, you got it easy from here on out. It's clear sailing, right up to the end.

I took a deep breath. I didn't want to ask. But I did. Want to ask.

Do I marry Angie?

She laughed.

Are you kidding me? What the hell kind of a nutty question is that?

I'm just wondering.

You're being silly, and you know it. What's she got to do with anything? No, you absolutely do not marry that girl. Ten years from now, you're going to look back and wish you never asked me that.

In a couple of weeks, I'm going in for an ultrasound. A couple of months after that, they'll be shipping me off to hospice.

She was probably right. I already felt like a heel for asking. I didn't like thinking about Angie that way. I don't know why I said it.

But I had more Angie questions. Maybe I had more Angie questions than me questions.

Is she in Europe?

Extra long pause. Long drag. She looked deep in the eyes. Squinted.

No.

Then…she's still here? She hasn't left yet?

Deep exhale of smoke.

How the Devil should I know? Come on, kid, this is *your* reading, not *hers.* You want someone else's reading? Get 'em in here, put 'em in the hot seat and I'll work my Polish magic. Right now, it's your turn, and I'm telling you, you got it made in the shade. Sweetie, I've been doing this for years. Not once did I get a customer that was about to hit the lottery. Not once. I wish Heavens to Betsy that my ship would come in and bring me a winner one of these days. No bluffing. But we don't all get the long straw. Honestly, kid, I'm happy as a pig in slop that I can tell you that you're not gonna get murdered in one of those awful drive-by shootings. Some poor kid's always getting caught up in one of those. It's such a pity. She waved it away. But not you, kid. Fifty so-so years, and you cash out in a warm bed. Trust me, you got dealt a fair hand. I'm even a little jealous.

I kick the bucket months before my grandchild's born. How's that for luck?

It's old news. Seen it coming for years. Believe me, sweetie, I had my pity party a long time ago. Now, I'm just fine. It's nothing; it's one page out of a book. What can I say? This is life.

Gosh, I said. I'm so sorry. She shrugged, waved it off with her cigarette hand.

She raised her voice, cocked her head over towards the living room. AND AT LEAST I AIN'T GONNA DO NOTHING STUPID LIKE SELL MY SOUL TO THE SHITFACED SATAN.

A voice yelled out from the bedroom, WOMAN, I'M WARNING YOU! I MEAN IT, FOR CRYING OUT LOUD! DON'T PUSH MY BUTTONS YOU'RE SKATING ON THIN WATER! YOU HEAR ME?!?

Never mind him, she said. What else you got for me?

How…how will I meet my wife?

She frowned. Now why on Earth would you want to know that? Kid, I just told you, nothing special's gonna happen. You want me to spoil everything? You don't wanna know everything.

She clasped her hands together. Okay, we're done here. Happy Birthday, Marius. That'll be eighty bucks. Cash, credit or debit?

But I'm paying—

IT'S THIN ICE YOU FRIGGIN MORON. THIN. ICE.
THIN WATER DON'T MAKE NO DAMNED SENSE.
OR DID YOU SELL YOUR BRAINS TOO?

WOMAN, I SWEAR TO—

SWEAR TO WHAT? WHAT, FRANKIE? SWEAR TO GOD?
HUH? YOU SANK THAT BATTLESHIP, HONEY.

FOR THE LOVE OF—WHY DO YOU ALWAYS HAVE TO—

YOU'RE A JOKE, FRANKIE, YOU KNOW THAT?

YOU GO TOO FAR, WOMAN. I GOT HALF A MIND TO
COME IN THERE AND—

YOU AIN'T GOT HALF A MIND, THAT'S THE
PROBLEM. Aw shucks, I'm sorry kid, this is unprofessional.
It's my husband. I'm sorry. He got drunk at the bar with some
old redheaded clown a few weeks ago. Cause of that, in a
couple months he's gonna go and blow half our savings at the
race tracks. I'm a little sore about it, is all. I won't be able to
stop him. That man, I—goodness, forget about it. What were
we talking about? Right. You. Yeah. The marriage thing.
No, no, listen, sweetie, it's your dime we're on, but trust
me, some things you don't wanna know. Sometimes, surprise
is the spice of the life.

I thought variety was supposed to be the spice of life.

Variety, surprise, whatever you like, sweetie.

The spice is all I'm saying.

I paid in cash. She lifted the bifocals from her chest to the tip of her nose, eyed the money narrowly, then stood up and left the room, counting the bills as she went.

As I made my way for the front door, a voice from the living room whispered pssst, kid. Hey, kid.

It was the old guy on the recliner. He was waving me over. I looked back at the dining room.

Empty.

I went into the living room. Dark place, dusty smell, cigarettes and whiskey, old furniture, nothing lit but the blue television glow. An old guy was sitting there on the couch, in boxers and a wife-beater, eating a bowl of cereal.

Don't listen to her, kid, he said. My wife's a liar.

She's a fake?

Whoa, whoa, he said. Ain't say all that. She's bona fide, alright. All's I'm saying is—hey, are you Amish or something? The hell you doing here?

I'm not Amish.

What's with the getup? Look like an Alabama preacher man.

 guess it was nice of her to not tell me, but at the same time, shouldn't I get a refund? She probably had me there, though.

Well, I'm not.

Whatever you say, compadre. My old man used to say, mine is not the reason why, but to do and die.

Anyhow, all I'm saying is, keep your wits about you. When Martha don't want to tell the truth, she makes shit up.

FRANKIE, FOR THE LOVE OF MERCY, WOULD YOU STOP HARASSING MY DAMNED CUSTOMERS!

I AIN'T HARASSING NOBODY! AND I MEANT THIN WATER, WOMAN! YOU THINK YOU CAN WALK ON WATER LIKE SOME KINDA, SOME KINDA WISE ASS—

I left.

And that was my psychic reading. It lasted all of twenty minutes and cost me eighty dollars.

Yes, I was pretty down about it for a long time after that. The very last thing that I expected to get was boring news. I thought I was guaranteed either a really exciting fortune telling or a really unfortunate one. Nothing special was just kind of extra fucky. I know a lot of people that never really do anything special in life, but, like… do they ever really think it's nothing special? Do you really get to sum up your whole life and think, "Eh, that was nothing special"?

But what if her husband was right? What if I am going to get shot in a drive-by, and she didn't want to tell me about it?

If I was caught in a drive-by, my last thoughts wouldn't be, hey, that psychic screwed me out of eighty bucks! Instead, I'd probably just think, boy, getting shot really hurts.

Plus, how am I supposed to get mad at her? If she was even partially telling me the truth, by now she's already dead. Like everyone, eventually. Like Nick.

Funny story about Nick, that kid I knew from grade school. Or not funny. You be the judge.

After I found out about his death, not even a month ago, I read up about him. He didn't have many friends, but after he died like fifty people all claimed to be his best bud. Everybody was blogging about him. He had major depression. Clinical, major depression, not just what everybody has. Even back in grammar school he was like that. Grammar school.

That's like a whole four years before being depressed turns into a cool thing. I remember, we were hanging out during recess and he told me that he felt like he was slowly disappearing. You know, becoming invisible. What a messed up thing for a fifth grader to think. But I had no idea what he was talking about. I was like, that's cool, you're like a superhero. I wish I could make myself invisible.

He didn't seem to think it was very cool.

Fast forward fifteen years or so. I read about this in a few blogs. That disappearing thing? He felt like that his whole life. down into the computer or something.

There's even a name for feeling that way, it's like a legitmate thing. After fighting with it for years, Nick went to see a psychiatrist.

Only the psychiatrist's secretary forgot to put the appointment down into the computer or something. When Nick went to see the therapist, the doors were closed Lights out. Nobody there. Oops.

It was pretty funny. Apparently he posted a bunch of stuff about it on the internet. Like, in a funny way. Ha ha, listen to this, everybody, it's so hilarious and ironic.

Then, two days later, he drove his station wagon into a quarry.

It wasn't so funny anymore.

I didn't really understand it at first, to be honest. I understand depression. I get that. Major depression must be the worst. Life is crummy enough on its own, without the chemicals in your head being all fucky.

But when you add crummy brain chemicals to an already crummy life, you don't stand a chance. But to want to end it all, just because you feel like nothing you do matters? Like nobody knows that you exist? I didn't understand that.

I get it now. I wish I didn't.

And that's how I ended up at the gas station. Five bucks into the Subaru and a pack of menthols. I always thought that menthols were the wussy cigarettes, but apparently they were supposed to be my favorites.

I guess I like the idea of menthols. It sounds like smoking a breath mint. That's cool. It'd be like a fun little twofer.

I had to buy a lighter too, because if I used the lighter in the car and mom found out I was smoking in the Subaru, she'd kill me.

I didn't know you guys were allowed to smoke, said the guy at the gas station.

I shrugged.

So there I was, outside the gas station. Cigarette in mouth. Lighter in hand. Hand shaking.

I thought, if the psychic was right about this stupid cigarette, maybe she was right about everything. If she was wrong, well. Hell. I didn't even know. Maybe she lied about everything.

I didn't want to be clear sailing. I didn't want to like cigarettes.

I thought, if Angie were here, we'd probably both smoke the whole pack together in like ten minutes, then spend the rest of the night puking in the park down the street from her aunt's house.

That made me smile. Then it made me want to cry.

I lit the cigarette.

A Bonafide Man

They say, before you die, your life flashes before your eyes.
The entire sum of days, all in a blink. This is untrue. You
glimpse only one moment, and by this moment, a man
determines his afterlife.

Harvey Brussels lay on his deathbed, emaciated, with his
wife's pale, pruned hand clasping his own. She murmured
comforting words, but all that he saw and heard was this:

*A promenade down the street, roundabout Randolph and State.
At the corner, a stone's throw from the subway, a legless,
scrap-clothed homeless man perched over a bit of sidewalk,
rattling the change in a plastic cup. As Harvey passed, he
thought, I've enough luck for half a dozen men; I can spare
some for this poor, unfortunate fellow. He dipped two fingers
into his inner breast pocket and drew out his lucky silver
dollar. It had the sparkle of his teeth and the sheen of his hair.
The coin was almost an organ. He scrutinized it a bit. For
anyone else, the coin represented approximately a hundred
pennies. To Harry, it ratified a wholesome marriage, an infant
daughter and dividends.*

*Flashing a millionaire grin, Harry flipped the silver dollar
into the homeless man's cup. A little luck, from a friend. We
can all use some, once in a while. He winked, in his mind.
He didn't lose cadence; he even felt extra spring in each
footfall.*

*Moments later, he felt a sharp stab at the back of his head.
Harvey spun around.*

*The homeless man, snarling, bearing fleshy gums, had
hurled the silver dollar back at him, then further extended
gratitude by saluting his middle finger out to the middle-aged
executive. Harry sized up the derelict carefully, then looked
down at the ground to see where his silver dollar lay. Then,
back up at his attacker. The man's eyes were drunken, wild
and bloodshot red. His gurgling, indiscernible language
expressed open hostility.*

*Silently, Harvey bent down and retrieved his silver dollar,
placing it back within his breast pocket. Without further
regard, he turned his heels and continued on his way.*

He never mentioned the incident to anyone, but it planted
the firm conviction within him to discontinue all dispense
of charity. He thought, a man who refuses good luck grants
entry to ill fortune. This statement became his new lucky
coin. He thought it a well-crafted, thought-provoking
statement. He often repeated it to his daughter Ramona,
though she was far too young to understand. That was okay.
One day, he thought, she will.

The hand held within Lynda Brussel's own suddenly went
limp. Lynda looked to her husband's glazed, vacant eyes.
His expression had changed; she could not read it. It could
be a smile, or not a smile. Perhaps ironic, perhaps malicious.
It was not satisfied. Or it searched for satisfaction.

Love Me Nicky Ocean

Let me tell you the hardest part first.

Everybody in the world knows about the O'Hare Massacre by now. A guy's wife and kid are deported back to Ecuador. The guy loses it. The guy gets hold of two semi-automatic weapons somehow and goes postal at the airport. Forty-eight dead. Thirty-six wounded. The guy points one of the guns to his forehead. BANG. The End.

I was there. I was number thirty-six. Shot clean through the shoulder blade.

At the time, I was sitting in a terminal and drinking an overpriced mango smoothie. This was before 9/11, when you could still walk around an airport without a boarding pass. There I was, sitting, people-watching and smoothie-drinking, and then there was a loud POP and people started falling. They were dominoes. They were toppling trees. They were suits shaken off hangers.

He shot the strawberry lady in the bright red jump suit. He shot the hipster girl with the knit hat and the tattoos. He shot the bald Eastern European guy with the white beard and the violin case. He shot the young Asian couple with the baby. Blood splattered in my hair and on my face and in my eyes and on my lips. I tasted hot copper. Then he was standing directly in front of me. I saw the gun. I saw the wild flames in his eyes and the foamed spit at the sides of his mouth. My legs froze and my mind froze and I didn't even hear the first gunshot as the bullet punched into my shoulder and then ripped back out of my shoulder.

184

Screaming and screaming and I wasn't screaming, but everyone else was screaming and I braced myself for the next bullet and okay here it comes and then someone dove in front of me and I closed my eyes and my knees buckled and

And for a long time after that, the painkillers were the only way that I could sleep. Not just because of the pain, although my shoulder hurt like a mother. Even now, I sometimes take sleeping meds because when I close my eyes I see his eyes. They are not human eyes. Grizzly bears probably have the same eyes when they are about to tear a man to pieces. I don't believe in the Devil and I only partially believe in God, but I one hundred percent believe in the horrible It that can possess people and animals and make them destroy everything around until there is nothing left. I want to believe that there is also something out there that is just as powerful and unstoppable, only good. I haven't seen anything like that yet.

The painkillers were a blessing. The painkillers were good. In the hospital they pumped me full of Demorol every four hours, and then it was goodbye terror, hello happy place. But then, when they started to wear off, there were the chills and the nightmares and the half-asleep daymares. Feeling blood on my arms when there was none. Still moments at the hospital room when I needed someone to hold me and tell me I wasn't going to die, I wasn't number forty-eight, it's okay, I'm alive and not dead and there's a difference... I would start gasping and having spasms, clenching the side rails along the bed and hoping that I wasn't losing my mind. I'd try to calm down enough to call the nurse and ask if it had been four hours yet. No? Damn it.

**

My mother came to visit once, after I was transferred to the CCU. It was awkward and brief. She sat in the chair facing the bed and kept looking at the clock. She crossed her legs, folded her arms and pinched her lips like she does. She seemed to need a cigarette badly. After about twenty minutes, she left without saying goodbye.

My ex-husband-turned-BFF Constantin came to visit twice. The first time he brought a Hallmark card that was probably very witty (I did not read it). He knelt by my bed, kissed my fingers and said in German, if you had died, my dear, I would have died with you. His English is perfect, but he always switches back to German when he gets really emotional. In the other visit, he stared out the window the whole time so that he wouldn't have to look at me. He smiled a plastic smile and he told me about the new guy he was dating. In the middle of a sentence a tear ran down his cheek and he said, verdammt noch mal, ich kann es nicht schaffen, and ran out of the room. He called every day after that, but did not come back.

My best friend Melly also came to visit once. She wore those tacky, huge, bug-eyed sunglasses so that I wouldn't see her cry. Right away she said I can't come back here, I'm sorry, I can't do it again, I just can't (her uncle Clark died of cancer in the same hospital; it hit her hard). Melly's Australian but I think she sounds like a pirate and I tease her about it all the time. Okay, everyone teases her about it. So I coughed and said in my terrible pirate voice arrrr, quite yer blubbering, gurly gurl. She told me to shut up and called me a fucken fuckhole. She's a sweet lady.

186

Even my sister Giulia came to visit, which was a shock since she thinks I'm a bitch. It was the shortest visit out of all of my visits. She acted like I was her old fifth grade teacher and not her big sister. Still, I could see that it had taken her a lot of nerve to show up. It was very nice to see that she cared at least a little that I was not dead.

A bunch more people called my hospital room to say hi and cheer me up and tell me how sorry they were. Everyone was there for me and so supportive and sweet in their own way. I felt so loved and at the same time nobody understood anything and when anyone talked it was like they were speaking an alien language, all chirps and clicks.

Maybe that was the painkillers at work. I don't know.

***

At the hospital, I got a bouquet of flowers. The card on it only said "Get well soon, A." I honestly thought the A was for asshole. My friends would do something like that; they are all adorable little jerks. But everyone that I asked just laughed and said no, ha ha, it wasn't me.

***

I stayed at the hospital for almost a month. It normally wouldn't have taken so long, but after they fixed the bullet wound I got a staph infection and had to stay longer. Staph infections are wacked out diseases that you only catch at hospitals. You can die from them. You can check-in with a broken toe and drop dead from a funky disease floating around the supposed place of healing. Merry Fucken Christmas.

Eventually, I was discharged and sent home. Shipped out with a prescription for Darvocet: twenty pills, one refill. Way lighter than what they were giving me in the CCU, but enough to keep me warm and cozy for a couple of weeks.

***

Constantin wanted me to stay with him. It was tempting. Constantin was the perfect man and once upon a time the perfect husband and if he had just stayed in the damned closet he would have kept on being the perfect husband. Instead, he became the almost perfect friend. I knew he would pamper me. He would have taken better care of me than himself. Half of the time. Then the other half of the time he would spend man-whoring and bringing home random hot guys to bang. It's depressing that my ex-husband can seduce every man alive, straight or gay, meanwhile we'd been divorced for two years and twenty-nine days and I haven't been out on a single date.

I told him no.

Then Melly said I should stay with her and her roommates The Anarchists. Now that might have been a hoot. They're all vegans and I'm a vegetarian. We got along famously, except for when I had to choose between my beliefs and my love for cheese. Then it was a battle. They think that being a vegetarian is fence sitting. The only thing that makes me a vegetarian and not a vegan is cheese. I fucken love cheese so much. I would stab a man in the belly for a pound of Roquefort. I will not stand by and listen to someone tell me that eating cheese is wrong.

I also fought with The Anarchists about how I worked at El Queso Conservatory. Though it was privately owned, The Anarchists only thought in terms of farmers and evil henchmen for the Capitalist Death Machine. I suppose they had a point there. Back in the good ol' days I was vegan and straight-edge and hardcore as hell and fucken punk fucken rock. Now I sell wine and cheese to yuppies. Guilty.

Apart from all of that, though, The Anarchists were cool company. Super smart. Way mellower than The Anarchists I used to know. If I'd moved in with them, we would've been a happy house full of aging punk train wrecks. Vegan potluck dinners. Movie nights. Roller derby. We could have borrowed each others' clothes and anti-depressants. Wee!

I told Melly no.

I wanted to be alone.

No. I wanted to be with someone who didn't ask questions. Someone who didn't look at me with eyes that said I want to help but I have no idea how to help. I wanted someone who didn't need an explanation, since everything that mattered couldn't be explained with words.

There was no such person. So I spent the time half-watching movies, staring at the walls, and downloading music that I had no intention of listening to. Oh, and dropping to the floor, curling up into the fetal position and hyperventilating. Did that a few times. It's not so fun.

I'm not a 'woe is me' kind of person. The last time I remember crying is when I was thirteen; in the middle of it, I screamed at my mom that she was the biggest bitch in the universe.

So I was more surprised than anything when, twenty years later, I became prone to hysteric fits of sobbing and shaking. Losing your shit is not really like it is in the movies. I wasn't thinking about the shooting every day. I was thinking about it, but I was trying really hard to block it out. One morning I would be going to get milk from the fridge, and the next thing I knew I'd be on the ground, choking and hacking and clawing at the ground and thinking holy Jesus, I'm having a heart attack. I'm going to die. This is happening this is happening this is happening.

I tried to tell myself, you'll get through this. This too shall pass. But nothing was passing. Every day was tough as shit.

I was lucky, at least, that I didn't have to work. My boss Mateo at El Queso Conservatory gave me a month off (on top of the three weeks at the hospital). It was unheard of, but I figured Mateo wanted to cut his losses in case I showed up and freaked out in front of the customers. I probably wouldn't have, not if I stayed medicated, but who knows? I was grateful for the time off, even though it was all unpaid and I had to dip into my security money to cover rent (I have a do-not-touch account from when my dad passed away years ago).

Constantin came by twice to stock me up with groceries. He bought all organic stuff that he said was supposed to cleanse and rejuvenate the mind, body and soul. Fucken wheat grass. Most of it went bad in the fridge.

Then, a few nights after I got home from the hospital, he showed up.

***

He is Viggo. I call him Viggo. The world knows him as Amazing Man. I glimpsed the newspapers and online stuff and watched the news, but like a lot of people I just thought it was all phony. He was supposed to be some insanely strong man that went around posing as a superhero. Only he was also a drunk and a cokehead and mostly caused property damage and got into trouble. There were movies and books about him. He was more of a burnt-out celebrity than a superhero.

Well one night I heard a tapping on my living room window, and there he was, this huge man the size of a grizzly bear, wearing a pine green hoodie and a red baseball cap brought down low to cover his eyes. If I hadn't popped three pills a half hour before, he would have scared the shit out of me. As it was, I stared at the window and thought, I better let him in, else he might break the window and come in anyway. I cracked open the window and asked, can I help you?

You that scary lookin' broad from the airport?

I stared. Blinked.

Yes?

It's me.

Oh is it now, I said. I had no idea who he was.

191

He reached down and lifted up his hoodie. Underneath was a grey spandex shirt with a big black letter A on it.

Are you an adulterer? I said.

He stared for a minute.

No, he said.

Sweet, I said.

I let him in.

That's really all there was to the introduction. You can cut a lot of corners while trashed on painkillers.

I didn't ask if he was a robber, rapist or serial killer. No, I saw fit to ask only if he were an adulterer. For some reason, the most important thing to me was to make sure that this mysterious midnight visitor practiced fidelity. If that isn't a solid argument against drug abuse than I don't know what is.

***

He said that he wanted to check up on me. See, he had been the one to jump in front of me at the airport. The bullets bounced off his chest and then just as he was about to grab the shooter and pound the fist of justice into him BANG.

It could have been Amazing Man's triumphant comeback. Instead, he was only another bystander.

A little later, I found out that he had attended the therapy group set up for the O'Hare Massacre survivors. Around the third or fourth meeting, they asked him to please stop attending.

Ungrateful sons a' bitches is what they are, said Viggo.

***

That first night, Viggo sat on the couch for about ten minutes and didn't say much. Then he got up and said I gotta go fight crime now, maybe I'll be back.

Viggo came back two nights later. Stayed another ten minutes. Equally awkward.

On the third night, as he was about to climb out the window I said dude, do you want to stay and watch a movie or something?

After that, he came by regularly. About three times a week. Always in the middle of the night. Always via fire escape. It was really funny to see him squeeze through the window. I kept waiting for him to get stuck, but he never did. I suppose he thought he was being incognito, despite being the eternal white elephant in the room. He was Definition: Conspicuous. The arch enemy of incognito. But he was old news now. The paparazzi did not chase him. A camera crew did not follow him around. I was not his latest mistress in the media (I checked). If we all have fifteen minutes of fame, then his fifteen minutes had long since gone by.

***

So wait, okay, I said, so when you say superhero, what do you really mean? Super as in strong? What is the super part all about? I was sitting on the couch and Viggo stood up and bent over a little and then with one hand lifted the couch way off the ground. My head bumped up against the ceiling. Then with his other hand he lifted up my cocktail table by one of the legs and then, holding up both the cocktail table and the couch with me sitting on it Viggo said if you want, I can juggle. I said please don't.

***

I am sure that Viggo wanted to sleep with me, but he never made a move and I certainly did not want him to make a move. He's sweet, but not really a looker and kind of a doofus. Plus, he was totally wasted almost every time I saw him. Weed or booze or heavier shit. He often showed up on the fire escape with coke powdered all over his pork chop mustache. If I'd have been in my right mind, I would have kicked him out or called the police. But I was very, very far from my right mind. So I let him stay, and we hung out together and watched movies. I have a weakness for cheesy romantic comedies; apparently, he did too. You would just automatically think that a guy like that is into football, but he got all giddy over rom coms. I would pop popcorn and douse it with parmesan and chili powder and Italian seasoning and we would begin our cheesy movie marathon.
Definition: Pleasure.

Sometimes, instead, he would come over with a case of beer and sit on my couch and drink the whole case without offering me a single can and go on and on about his day.

Sometimes it was really exciting. Other times, I would turn on my computer and tune him out and surf the net. He didn't even seem to mind. He was just happy to be around.

***

I told him up front that I wasn't going to have sex with him, not ever. Not in a million years. Not in a trillion years. Not even if someone put a gun to my head and said either do it with a fat vigilante or die. I might have been a little harsh about it. I can't even blame it on the pills. I'm just like that—though I'm not nearly as hardcore as I used to be. But if it hurt his feelings, he didn't show it.

You ain't my type, he said, I don't go for you Halloween-looking broads. Not this fat Sicilian. I'm from New York.

He's not even Sicilian. He's a mutt like every other American. His father was half Polish and half German. His mother was half Italian and half Romanian. Somehow, Viggo thought that made him Sicilian. Your guess is as good as mine.

***

We ordered pizzas. We watched lots of television. We played cards and Scrabble and he sucks hard at cards and Scrabble. He drank himself stoopid all the time and passed out on my couch, my bathtub, my kitchen floor and my walk-in closet. The closet was the worst one: he walked into it—thinking it was the bathroom—and peed on the floor before passing out. I stopped using said closet.

Let me say it again: he did NOT hit on me. Not once.

He was wasted most of the time and awkward and he broke my coat hanger and my medicine cabinet mirror and one leg of my cocktail table, and he clogged the toilet constantly— but he never once hit on me. Now and then he would peek at me from the side of his eyes and one extremely gross time he was talking about lord knows what and down below I could see his little guy standing salute from underneath his pants, right out there in attack mode like, oh hai, I'm Viggo's erection, don't mind me, I'm just goin' hang out here with y'all for a minute, k thnx bye.

But he never did anything about it.

I am pretty sure he downloaded porn on my computer while I was sleeping though. I'm almost positive. But that's too nasty for words and thinking about it makes me want to vomit. I didn't know how to mention it. I couldn't have said hey Viggo, please don't look at porn on my laptop and especially don't do whatever it is you're doing while watching porn on my laptop. But then if he said okay, sure thing, it meant that he had been downloading porn on my laptop and that was disgusting in so many ways and I could never again have used my computer or sat on my computer chair or sat near the desk or around the desk or in that region of the room ew ew ew ew.

It's so weird. Years ago I would have been done with a guy like him after five minutes. In many, many ways he represented the kind of male that I hated with a passion for most of my life. He even looked a little like this scummy rapist dudebro that I totally beat the crap out of back in college.

I think that's important to stress that.

One of the driving reasons for me moving out of the country
in the first place was because I wasn't attracted to women but
I wanted some kind of assurance that it was just the men in
this country that sucked so hard and not men all over the
world. And here now was me and here was Viggo and he
looked like the mascot for shitty patriarchal Amerikkka
and somehow I did not hate his guts.

***

We swapped famous people stories. Ha. No. Viggo told me a
bunch of his celebrity stories, and then afterwards I threw in
my little two cents. Viggo had met a ton of people, saved a lot
of CEOs and politicians and movie stars. He'd gotten trashed
and wrecked hotel rooms with rock stars. However, I had
only one story. When I was going to college in Tallahassee,
or shall I say before I dropped out of college in Tallahassee,
I bartended to make extra money. Heinrich Herz used to
hang out at my bar all the time. Remember him, Heinrich
Herz? The boy genius from the eighties? He grew up to
become a sleazy little shit. Definition: PIG. He was the worst.
And I used to idolize him, just like every other kid on
the planet. We all thought he was a ticking time bomb of
potential, just waiting to explode and POOF! A New Earth.
Only he didn't explode. He didn't even implode. His star
faded. His great contribution to the world was to knock up a
few unlucky ladies and/or spread around venereal diseases.
Definition: Tragic.

Viggo had better stories. You can read some of them online,
but there are also a lot of great stories that the media didn't

That was a big marketing scam. Some movie studio wanted to stage "real life" action scenes for Amazing Man, so that they could build a franchise around it. They spent a few million on these black market killer robots that Amazing Man was so obviously going to defeat... and then they followed that up by spending hundreds of millions of dollars on Amazing Man movies, cartoons, comics, and toys. The scandal came out, but the company was so smart about it that nothing could be legally traced back to them.

Red tape like that pissed Viggo off. In the beginning he wanted to be like a comic book superhero. That sure didn't work out. Everyone he 'defeated' usually went on to sue him blind. In the end, he could only go after small time crooks, purse snatchers, and petty thieves. He didn't go after drug dealers because many of them were his suppliers. Mostly, he stuck to intervening in big freak accidents. That was his bread and butter. He was that kind of superhero. Too many legal complications involved in fighting crime.

I must say, it was cool to hear him talk about real-life superhero problems. He had a real thick New York accent. Just to look at him, you would have thought he was a greasy mechanic or a plumber. And most of what came out of his mouth was pretty asinine. But then on a roll he'd say things that I wouldn't have expected. Stories about the UN, or Cambodia. He would get all worked up about it. You know what the problem is, he'd say. All the rotten bastids out there are running the show. Can't go after the real baddies. Those lousy bastids make the laws. They put on a big game, but they ain't fooling me. Nuh-uh. Not this fat Sicilian. Listen to this—

cover. You know those huge robots that caused all that
damage to downtown Chicago? And on and on.

**

Once I told him, hey, I'll be your sidekick. All I need is a
costume. You can call me The Spinster. My super power is
warding off men. All types of men. I can even turn straight
men gay. Viggo suddenly got quiet and said hey, that's not
cool, you shouldn't say shit like that.

I'm wasn't sure if he was being culturally sensitive or
homophobic.

I said I'm sorry, I don't really have gay-making powers.

I know that, he said. I ain't dumb. Anyway, I don't need no
sidekick no way. I already had one. He came up short.

Oh.

I looked it up later: Mega Boy, aka Felix Mendelstein,
sidekick slash pro-bono attorney slash agent slash chaperone.

He was number forty-eight.

**

I think Viggo was molested as a kid. Almost positive. He
wasn't a homophobe and he never went off on any lame
gay bashing or anything, but whenever gayness was the
topic of the night he got really Definition: Serious and
spoke in hushed tones.

Man that could be like a punch line to a joke: ha ha, the superhero was molested as a kid. But it's not funny, it's so darned sad. Imagine it: this little boy with the power of a hundred men burning inside him, too scared to budge and letting some filthy scum have his way.

**

Okay, said Viggo, here we go. Fiddy questions. You're lucky as hell. Friggin newspapers would pay out the nuts for this. All access. Ask me anything.

What's your favorite country?

America. Only place I been.

You don't like to travel?

Planes give me the heebie-jeebies.

Then why the hell were you at the airport?

Lots of people at the airport. Somebody gonna try and break the law.

Do you have a weakness?

Fuckin' Philly cheesesteaks, oh my friggin—

No, a real weakness. An Achilles heel. Kryptonite. Something that steals your power.

Beets. Taste like shit. Next question.

How did you get your super powers?

He shrugged.

Were you born with them?

Shrugged.

Did your parents have any super powers?

Viggo frowned.

You mean, like, powers they never told nobody about?

Yeah.

Nope.

What did your parents do?

Ol' man was a butcher.

And your mother?

Butcher's wife.

They never did anything… amazing? Superhero-ish?

Viggo glanced up at the ceiling. Scratched his head.

There was this time, Ma was gonna stabs the old man.
Right inna middle a' dinner.

He was eating, she just come up behind, yanked him by the hair and put a meat cleaver to his friggin' throat.

Screaming at him. Old man starts bawling like a little girl. Never seen nothing like it before.

What did your mother do?

Dropped the knife and walked back into the kitchen. Guess she proved her point.

And did you ever find out?

Find what out?

What your father did? To make your mother nearly slit his throat?

Viggo shrugged.

He shrugged a lot. It was his main thing. Shrugging.

***

It wasn't all shrugs and roses, though. Occasionally, I'd be in a mood or he'd be in a mood and the night would just go sour. He would show up and be visibly bothered and in the middle of the night he would just break down, hide his face behind his huge hairy hands and start crying. I don't know if it was the drugs or the booze or what, but he'd just start bawling. No it wasn't bawling, it was weeping. It was soft and quiet. The way a small child sounds.

When he did that, I didn't know what to do.

He'd say the same thing over and over. I didn't save them, I didn't save none of them. It ain't my fault. I didn't mean to do it.

I didn't know if he meant the people at the airport or something else entirely.

At those moments, I should have hugged him, rubbed his back or told him it was all going to be okay. But all I ever did was sit and stare.

***

One night, he pulled his wallet out of his pocket, took out a small photo. It was black and white, blurry and clipped out of a newspaper.

See this, he said. This is why I do what I do.

He handed me the picture.

I was at the bar with my bud Horton, and he says to me, he says, a fella should always keep a picture in his wallet. Picture of someone more important than him. Let him know who he's out there fighting for. Can be anybody. Long as they matter.

I looked at the picture.

Oh snap, I said. I knew her. Kind of. Not really. She was my sister's friend.

I had known her, although not very well. She was my sister's friend from college. Maybe more than friend.

I don't know. It was suspect. But the girl was loco; she jumped in front of a subway train one day, completely out of the blue. No phone call. No letter. Nothing.

I was on that train, said Viggo. Passed out in the last car. Fucken Christian Brothers. You know how easy it is for me to stop a moving train? Easy as shit. Pardon my French. If I'da known—

There was no way you could have known, I said. She wanted to die.

Viggo looked at me and his eyes were glassy and spilling over onto his cheeks and he said,

The hell would anybody wanna die for?

He seriously didn't get it. At all. Total emptiness. He took the photo and slipped it back into his wallet. Wiped his eyes.

No fucken way, he said. Sorry. No effen way. Shaky voice. Not on my watch. Not this fat Sicilian.

Tears.

At least I saved you, he said. I saved you real good.

I didn't feel as though anyone had saved me from anything. Not from the blood and not from the bullet and not from the thoughts and the It; the It had stained me and the stain could not be washed away.

Yes, I said. You did.

Around that time, I got a letter in the mail from my cousin Casper (he doesn't 'do' email). He was living in Spain. Well really, he was kind of a nomad. But he was living in Spain for the time being. He wanted me to fly out there and stay with him. I wanted to, but I didn't have the money. Not without dipping into my security money, which I didn't want to do. And I made chump change at El Queso Conservatory. All it did was feed my cheese addiction and just barely keep me from getting evicted. The security money was the only safety net I had in case I got laid off, sick, or something else majorly cruddy happened. But Casper was persuasive. He said that all I had to do was buy the plane ticket. He lived in an a flat with six other people. It was their own happy commune, a crummy crash pad for aging skater punks. All they did was work odd jobs to make ends meet so that they could spend the rest of the time skating, playing music and being grubby. If I could only forget about privacy and clean spaces—and the fact that I'm thirty-four—it would be the perfect medicine.

I mailed him back a sheet of loose-leaf notebook paper with two words written on it:

Not yet.

Airports terrified me. The same way that hospitals terrify Melly. Buying a plane ticket was fine and getting on an airplane was fine and so was taking off and staring out the window and seeing everything get smaller and smaller. That was all fine. But walking around the airport and seeing so many pink and brown fleshy bodies and imagining them all sagging and bloody and piled up on the ground, collapsed on the moving escalators with their eyes wide open and full of death—that was not fine. That was very, very not fine.

Which is ironic; the reason I was at the airport that day was that airports were my happy places. I didn't have the means to fly away, so I went to the airport to relax, people-watch and spend a few hours feeling as though I were on the verge of re-setting my life in a new place. Airports made me feel like one small piece of a big, beautiful, unfinished painting. Everyone at the airport was about to travel, or coming back from traveling, or seeing off a traveler. It was this big awesome circus full of travelers, all kinds of different people linked with one purpose: travel.

Airports stayed that way, always, whatever the time and whatever the day.

That was what I thought before. Afterwards, airports only meant bloody death.

Instead of hanging out with bloody death, I took my pills and hung out at my apartment with my superhero.

***

We usually stayed at the apartment, but every now and then, when it was really, really late, we went out. Neither of us wanted to be around a lot of people so we only went to quiet places, or places owned by people who owed Viggo favors. Despite being socially inept, Viggo had actually saved a whole lot of people, so a whole lot of people felt like they owed him big time. There was this Korean karaoke bar. The owner let Viggo come in whenever he wanted to, even during closed hours. A couple years ago, Viggo rescued a school bus from colliding with a train, and the owner's daughter was on the bus.

Out of gratitude, the owner gave Viggo an unlimited karaoke pass. So we went there and I would sit quietly and Viggo would sing awful power ballads. If you want to call it singing. Once or twice the Korean girls that worked at the place would come and join us. They would sing Korean pop songs and Viggo would mouth the lyrics and sound Definition: Awkward. I mean practically tone deaf. AND he didn't speak a word of Korean. He'd beg me to join him in a duet and I would get up from the couch and mumble gibberish into the microphone and let his big walrus voice drown me out.

Then he would crash into a table. Or break glasses. Or fall into the monitor and bust the screen. Or throw up everywhere. The owner would get pissed and shout in Korean and kick us both out, but we could always come back. He would never have banned Viggo from karaoke.

Fun, fun, fun.

There was other stuff though. He took me to this comic book store where late at night all the nerds would get together to play their lame role playing games. Viggo loved it, he would get together with these teenagers and pretend to be elves and wizards, rolling dice and battling imaginary dragons. I'd sit by the wall, watch, and try not to get any of the geekiness on my pants.

But even then every so often, Viggo would go off the deep end. He'd roll a two instead of a ten, or get lost in the Castle of Forbidden Magic. He'd yell out this is such bullshit and slam his fist against the table, breaking it in half.

Or one kid would make a wisecrack and he'd grab the poor nerd by the scruff of the neck and snatch him off his chair and high into the air, ready to whoop ass. The game master would shout Viggo! What the hell dude! Let it be, he's not even a level three air warlock! Viggo would huff and puff and then come to his senses and things would go back to normal.

Okay, I have to admit: maybe it was because most of the time I was loopy and half-asleep, but I started to get into role playing. Watching it; not playing it. Watching it was kind of rad. Or at least it had potential to be rad. It was nerdy and dumb and I would never do it, but it was really just a bunch of friends hanging out—not so different from watching a movie or playing a board game. You make up a new world, one much more beautiful than the real one, and you pretend to live in it with all of your friends. It's not hard to see the attraction.

***

We did so much together. Viggo brought over this video game system and when we couldn't think of anything to do, he would turn it on and play. This will probably not be a surprise to you but all of the games were about superheroes.

I wasn't interested in video games, but the Darvocet could make anything tolerable.

***

Being with him, it made me think of something my mom told me back when we were on speaking terms.

208

Way before Giulia was born, I had an imaginary friend. A monster. It showed up just after my dad passed away and mom started dating Doug-o the dirty fucken sex offender. Then it got sick and died. It wasn't what you would call a subtle behavioral issue. But it wouldn't have been so bad, except that I was past the age when imaginary friends are okay. Also, I talked about my monster buddy like it was real. I wrote about it for a home work assignment (my mom kept the paper and showed it to me ten years later: spooo-ky). I had to talk to social workers and psychologists. They put me on Ritalin and a few other things and, to make a short story shorter, I forgot everything. To this day, I can remember as far back as when I was five, but the imaginary monster friend is a black hole in my memory.

Even so, Viggo made me nostalgic in an odd way. As big and smelly and stoned as he was, I felt like I'd known him all my life. He was my big crusty protector, always there, maintenance free and never asking me for anything. I often wanted to just throw my arms around him and hug him and cry and sometimes I did all of that. Minus the crying.

Everything was perfect. It wasn't going to stay perfect and I knew it.

***

It was raining. Two in the morning. Viggo stood on the fire escape and wouldn't come in.

My shrinks say you ain't good for me, said Viggo. They say you nurture my self-destructive tendencies.

Is this a joke? Who says I nurture what now?

They'll only keep seeing me if I quit hanging out with you.

And you said no?

Viggo shrugged.

Viggo, you told them no, right?

What was I supposed to do? Tell them go to hell? You don't freaking understand, I'm getting sued out the a-hole by like thirty different a-holes. Every a-hole out there wants a round with this fat Sicilian. Everybody looking for a piece of Viggo cake. My lawyers, every a-hole on Team Viggo gonna take a walk if my shrinks tells me go eff myself. And then half a' those a-holes gonna turn right back around and sue my balls off. 'Excuse me. Pants off. I gotta show all them freakin' jokers that I ain't no psycho.

Viggo, what are you telling me? Say it.

We can't be friends no more.

Fine. Go away.

I shut the window.

I thought I was going to either laugh or cry but I did neither and stared at the wall and felt every inch of the nothingness that drowned the whole apartment and outside of the apartment and everywhere else.

I stopped listening to my voice messages. They piled up.
Mostly Melly and Constantin, but other friends too. There
were knocks on the door; I didn't answer them. Pills every
few hours. When the Darvocet ran out I took Tylenol and
when the Tylenol ran out I took aspirin and when the aspirin
ran out I thought about buying a jar full of extra-strength
sleeping pills and swallowing them all at once with glass
of orange juice.

I stopped showering. I put my blanket and pillow on the floor
next to the couch and slept on the hardwood floor.

I'm sure I looked like hell. Luckily my medicine cabinet
mirror was broken so I didn't have to see myself.

***

When it didn't matter anymore, I learned the missing parts
of the story about Viggo. Online. He didn't have a choice.
He'd fucked up so much that the state and federal government
wanted to do lock him down once and for all. For instance,
one time Viggo tried to stop bank robbers by throwing a
station wagon at them. It missed the robbers completely
but crashed into a flower shop and killed a guy. And that
was only one of countless fuck-ups. Even apart from what
he specifically did, there were all these other lawsuits. Angry
parents out for revenge because their kids thought that they
could be superheroes. One kid burned down his father's
furniture store because he thought his super power was
fire-starting. The boy said he was testing out his super powers,
so he could grow up to be just like Amazing Man. Lawsuit.

A regular person would've been sentenced to life in prison for any number of the things Amazing Man got away with. But the problem is that a penitentiary doesn't mean a whole lot to a guy who can bend steel and punch through walls. A new maximum security prison would have to be created specifically for Amazing Man, and that would cost millions of dollars. When you add to that the fact that, when he wasn't being a bull in a china shop, Amazing Man did actually save people—and lots of rich, important people—the only answer was rehabilitation.

Funny, I spent so much time with him that, in my head, he was mine. My superhero. It was easy to forget that he was everyone else's too.

Reading about it online didn't much change the way I felt. I was never really mad at him. Lost. Alone. Empty. But not mad.

***

Here's the part where I want to say that I had an epiphany, a turning point, a breakthrough that changed me and helped me keep on fighting. Sorry. There was no such breakthrough. The truth, be it good or bad, is that you can continue living your life with nothing to show for it. You may not have a reason to live, but you also don't have a reason to die. Eventually, you have to do something. It's a lazy feeling on a Sunday afternoon, groggy and yawning, when you lay in bed and don't want to move. Only it lasts for minutes and then hours and then days. Suddenly, you say to yourself, I have to get up. Nothing has changed but I have to get up.

If anything helped me make up my mind for me, it was re-reading three sentences written by my favorite writer in the world, Cindy Crabb. Hardly anyone in the world knows who Cindy Crabb is. That makes her the genius who is all mine. Whenever I meet someone who does know who Cindy Crabb is, that person is all mine too. When I read those three sentences, I knew that I was going to have to scrape myself up off the ground and fly away:

"But there was a time when my friends started dying, and there was a time when my friends started standing in the back of the room during the shows and then leaving. And I retreated somewhat too, because there was a part of myself I had to rescue. And now that it was rescued, now that it was flourishing, I wondered what it would be like, out there."

***

I mailed Casper a sheet of loose leaf notebook paper with three words scribbled on it:

I'm coming over.

***

The first step was to call Constantin and borrow two thousand bucks from him. I should not say borrowed. He owes me way more than two thousand dollars. I paid for the divorce and apart from that, he owed me over ten grand. I had to dip into my security money to loan it to him. Now he makes triple what I make, but because he's so sweet all the time I never tried to stick my hand in the cookie jar. But now I had a plan. I told him my plan to move back to Europe.

He promised to give me the money and then got weepy and went on about how sorry he was that he hadn't been there for me, even though I hadn't given him much of a chance.

After that, I called Melly and apologized for being a terrible friend. She accepted my apology in the calm, polite voice she uses when she's royally pissed off. I told her my plan and she called me a selfish cunt and hung up.

She called back fifteen minutes later and we talked for two more hours and by the end, everything was okay.

Then I called El Queso Conservatory and told Mateo that I was quitting my job and moving to Spain. He screamed and called me an ingrate, then cooled down and admitted that he'd replaced me months ago and never really considered taking me back. He was relieved that I wasn't calling to ask for my job back because that would've made for an awkward conversation. But I know, underneath the mean exterior, Mateo's a softy; when I come back, if I come back, I could probably get my old job back if I want it. I'm not sure I'll ever want it back, though.

Mateo wished me the best and said to let him know if I was going to go to Toledo because he would tell his cousins about me and I could stay with them. He assured me that they were very nice and wouldn't try to touch me. He was even a little too insistent about how nice they were and how they wouldn't dare touch me and it made me never want to meet his pervy cousins or set foot in Toledo ever.

The last person I called was my mom. I told her my plan and she said big whoop, you left me a long time ago. Dial tone.

***

Now here's the good part:

I searched newspaper after newspaper. Hours of searching.
Then I found an article about a young man who drove his
station wagon into a quarry. I read the whole article and then
I read more articles online. He was just a Definition: Sad little
ghost who couldn't find his way in, so he found a way out.
Probably nobody even cared except his family.

I found a picture of him in a magazine and cut out said
picture. There he was: Nicholas Ocean. He was a forgettable
looking young guy with a forgettable looking face. He could
be anybody at all.

On the back of the picture I wrote *I love you, Nicky Ocean.*
Then I folded up the photograph and tucked it into my change
purse.

Nicky Ocean, I'm sorry, you couldn't find a reason to live.
If it helps, you will be my reason. It's too late, but I want you
to know—I understand. I get you. I will keep your picture
forever and I will love you in a way that I will not describe
because it is a love that should not be trapped inside syllables.

***

I took a deep breath and bought my plane ticket. I took
another deep breath and dipped into my security money to
pay my rent for the next three months. I took a third deep
breath and packed everything I could into two suitcases.

215

I started freaking out as I left the apartment and continued to freak out as the train shipped me to the airport. I was even freaking out as I dragged my luggage out of the train and walked to the airport, hoping I wouldn't pass out along the way.

But then right near the entrance to the international terminal by the check-in there was Viggo sitting on the ground next to the benches, Indian style and awkward. He looked ragged and washed-up and hobo-ish, wearing a dirty flannel that wasn't buttoned up and showed his superhero costume underneath.

He saw me and I saw him and his eyes opened wide and he stomped over to me and his bear hug lifted me high into the air with my feet dangling out. I was supposed to still be mad at him, or at least pretend to be mad at him but right then I was free of everything I was supposed to be. Free of anger. Free of memories. I did not want to be mad and I did not want to pretend.

I asked him what he was doing at the airport and he said what the hell do you think, I come here every day. Rust don't sleep, and neither do Amazing Man.

I didn't know what that meant, but he said it in a very heroic way.

He also looked stoned out of his mind.

What do your shrinks say about this, I asked. Is this healthy? Did they tell you to come here? Wait—are you even allowed to talk to me?

Viggo shook his head.

Screw those Fascist sons a' bitches. I'm the goddamned Amazing Man. I can do anything. Pardon my French.

He took my hand and held it at check-in and then after check-in. He even bought a cheap plane ticket so that he could go into the terminals with me. The only time he let my hand go was when we had to pass through the metal detectors, and then he took my hand right back on the other side.

We found my gate and sat together at two of the seats by the wall. Viggo kept holding my hand while we sat and said, see, you're still alive.

I knew I would be in the clear once I boarded the plane, but I hadn't boarded the plane and at any moment there would be blood and brains and skin dripping down the walls and on me and from me and shrieking and dead eyes and

We sat and waited. And waited. And waited. I leaned my head against his arm and it was like leaning against a tree. A solid, massive, redwood tree. The tree was not going to topple. My tree was big and hairy and smelled like crud and body odor and I felt completely safe. And we sat there and waited and waited and waited and then it was time to board the plane.